AF278738

Three Pointers

a novel by

J. W. Wheeler

Copyright 2019 J. W. Wheeler
San Diego, Ca

Cover art and inside layout by: Tonja Daniels

The right of J. W. Wheeler to be identified as the author of this work has been asserted in accordance with the Copyright, Designs and Patents Act 1988.

This book is copyright material and must not be copied, reproduced, transferred, distributed, leased, licensed or publicly performed or used in any way except as specifically permitted in writing by the author, as allowed under the terms and conditions under which it was purchased or as strictly permitted by applicable copyright law. Any unauthorized distribution or use of this text may be direct infringement of the author's rights and those responsible may be liable in law accordingly.

This is a work of fiction and any resemblances between the characters and persons living or dead is purely coincidental.

Dedication

This book is dedicated, first and foremost, to Dr. James Naismith, the inventor of the game I love. Secondly, to the many millions of players on countless thousands of unsupervised courts who developed and evolved the good doctor's creation into the sport we now know. It was transformed by those who played it - not by coaches, Analytics or marketing strategies.

To all teachers everywhere, including those who have enriched me along the way: Dr. E. Neville Pickering, Brenda Dilts, Charles Schwalm, and the many others who have added their potion to my mix.

This book is also dedicated to James Joyce - and all the artists, poets, and writers who inspired him to create "A Portrait of the Artist as a Young Man" – and to those of us fortunate enough to have read it and know we can never aspire to reach such heights, but are inspired to try nonetheless.

To Ken Sailors and Bob Cousy, to Goose, Meadowlark, and Curly, to Tiny and Wilt, to the Iceman, the Doctor, the Hawk, the Pearl, to Bird and Magic, to Oscar and Clyde, to Bernard King and Hal Greer and John Havlicek, to Nique the Freak and His Airness.

And lastly, this book is dedicated to all those who thrive inside their own contradictions. Those enlightened by embracing the incompatibilities, not merely accepting them. The ones who rejoice in being uniquely human, never wasting their precious time and energy deforming themselves to conform to what is deemed normal. Those who know creativity is anchored into the edges and tears. I salute you and happily commiserate.

Acknowledgements

Thanks to Sue for the editing, Tonja for the bookmaking, Theo for the webmaster skills, and Kai, Jasmine, and Tia for putting up with me. To all of you who read this expecting something different, please forgive me. I promise to do better next time.

1. The Sweetness

Jimmy Williams was in love. Gloriously, confidently, totally besotted, his heart and soul filled with all the passion and wonder only true love could beget, each day an opportunity to proclaim and exclaim his devotion to an uncaring world. Willing to sacrifice, to endure whatever pain it may bring, to smile in the faces of those who ridiculed him for his constant declarations, his unabashed boldness, to overcome the limitations of his existence, to soar above the clouds without a parachute or any other means by which to safely land. Enough to happily laugh at the hatreds inside him that constantly schemed to separate him from his beloved and ignore those older and wiser who warned him of its eventual demise. Enough to envision the future and its bleakness, to revise the past to fit his preconceptions, and to live in peace with the present in the arenas available to him to prove what he knew deep in his core to be true.

And that was why even though his frail body was disinclined to run, he had no choice. He could not allow it to betray him, to allow the world to conclude his love could not compete with his fatigue when the most important questions were asked, when winning or losing depended on his ability to take the next step and not stand idly by, to not depend on others to deliver to him what he knew he did not deserve unless he took for himself.

He was breathing deeply now, focusing on each breath to control it precisely, to ignore the searing pain in his chest from the effort of that very act, to ignore the muscles in his thighs screaming for more oxygen as he took in each morsel of air, to ignore the cries of his swollen toes as they were hammered by the floor with each step. It was the only way he knew how to meditate; the only way he knew how to detach his mind from the gravity of the reality of his life, to loosen the shackles of his existence, the only way he could force himself to circle the track twenty times, a tenth of a mile per circuit, making turn after turn on the spongy track that hugged the inside of the outer wall of the YMCA building a few blocks from his parents' house.

He ran past the front entrance, six steps above him, and saw the glass doors covered in condensation, evidence of the frozen air outside and the steamy humidity within. After a few strides he glanced to his left and surveyed the open section which made up half of the Y's main floor - sometimes sectioned for multiple uses at the same time, be it tennis, wrestling, or little kids playing under a parachute - and sometimes for the same purpose, like two small basketball courts for the youngsters or one large court for the older guys. As he made a left turn, one of the eighty he would make before he completed the task he had set for himself, traveling parallel to what would have been the full sized court if it had been so configured, he noticed he had the gym almost to himself, like he did on most of the cold winter days he was spending in Canton until the last of his college winter breaks had run its course. He felt all alone traveling counterclockwise in circles, and wondered why humans and cars and horses everywhere run counterclockwise, with the lone exception being the horse tracks of Europe. Then he smiled to himself, realizing his college training must be nearing completion, because only an engineer would be thinking such things at such a time and be driven to research it later, which he knew he would.

Twenty times around the track. Every day except Christmas and Sundays from December 12nd, 1980, until this day, January 6th, 1981, Jimmy had been circling this track, thinking random thoughts. After another left turn at the far end of the court he returned to reality as he passed through the dark and dangerous passage below the locker rooms above. The danger requiring Jimmy to remain alert came not from muggers or hidden traps, but from randomly darting children with towels dripping water who could appear at any moment and cause a nasty fall. Unlike some of the grouchy old men who ran on the same track, Jimmy could not afford, literally, to complain about it. He had not been a member of the Y for years, going back to junior high school, seven or eight years before. For the last four years he had not even been living in Canton, except when the school closed the dorms between semesters and he didn't have a summer job in Chicago. After this, his fourth and last year of college and final winter break, he would not spend this much time in his home town or at his parents' home ever again. That thought alone filled him with awe.

As he cleared the dark passage and breathed in a large volume of air, filled with water vapor and chlorine, he smiled at his good fortune and discipline as he strode into the light pouring down from the ceiling above the pool which made up the other half of the main floor of the Y. He had a purpose. Before he left school after the fall semester ended he had realized he couldn't just lie around for a month and allow his muscles to atrophy. He couldn't do what he had done in the winter holidays before, to play occasional pickup games with his lazy boyhood buddies and watch his fitness melt into a toneless mass. Before he returned for his last term at Bradley University he would use this time to increase his current fitness level, to improve his conditioning, to do all he could to avoid being left gasping for breath late in the second half like had happened in the past.

His good fortune was to live close enough to walk to the Y when the weather cooperated, and not need to burn much precious gas to drive there when it didn't. He wore two thick flannel shirts over his sweat suit, and his big heavy winter coat, and left them hanging on the coat rack next to the entrance. Then he would immediately step down to the track level, instead of up to the front desk, so he could avoid the reality of not being an actual, paid member of the Y, and begin running. At the end of his twenty laps he would sit on the edge of the track and cool down, then return to the coat rack, button each layer and pull up his hood, and drive or walk home without showering. College kids in love did what they had to do.

Another left turn took him lengthwise past the pool, where several children were splashing and laughing as they bobbed up and down in the chemical mix they had added their bodily fluids to. Some would yell and wave as Jimmy bounced past, not caring if they swallowed a mouthful of the funny tasting water. The last left in the circuit led to the front of the building, covered, but not nearly as dark as the passage in the back, partly illuminated by the light from the glass doors streaming down either side of the stairway. As he passed under the front stairs Jimmy counted seven and then went on to the next circuit and his thoughts.

As soon as his hands touched the ball he made his move. The 2 – 3 zone they were facing had stifled everything else, and he had to try to break out of the cage his team was trapped in. As the point guard, it was his duty to distribute, to turn passes into open shots and free throws, but he knew he had to revert to his truer nature this trip down the floor. They had been passing the ball around the perimeter in vain, looking for an opening the zone would not provide as they had the last few times they had possession of the ball, but this time, Jimmy had something else in mind.

Standing at the top of the key, he passed to the wing as had been the pattern, but then he stepped forward, positioning himself closer to the two men facing him at the top of the zone, crouching at each corner of the free throw line, and stuck his right leg forward even further, putting it as close to in between his opponents as he could, so when the return pass touched his fingers he had to lean back to catch it. This, to Jimmy, was the riskiest part of the whole thing, catching the ball cleanly, so he could make his first move before the defense could react to stop him. He had purposely put the right foot forward, something he had learned, like so many others on his journey of devotion, on the playground. When you are too slow to split two defenders trying to double team you on a drive to the basket, get a head start by sticking your foot out to split them before you catch the ball in the first place. Once he secured the ball he stepped forward, a big step, with his left foot and pushed the ball toward the floor with his right hand. Thus, in one swift motion, he had moved past the top two guys in the zone.

However, the big boys from TKE house were playing a zone for this exact reason. They didn't have anyone quick enough to stop Jimmy Williams one on one. As soon as Jimmy stepped through, into the middle of the zone at the free throw line, the TKE center, all six foot six, two hundred twenty pounds of him, stepped forward to greet five foot eleven and three quarters, one hundred and thirty-five-pound Jimmy. Yes, thought Jimmy, come on up here, where I want you. The key to this move, and the reason why the catch and first step had to be clean, was Jimmy knew he needed to take two dribbles to make this all work. One dribble and he'd be eating leather. The first dribble had to be from his right hand to his left, even though he was moving straight ahead, so the ball would be in his left hand for the second dribble.

As the big man advanced, Jimmy planted on his left foot and watched the ball bounce into his left hand. The mountain in front of him completed his big step and was taking another to widen his base and cut Jimmy off. Repeating a move he had made so many times he had forgotten when he lost track, he took a long stride with his right leg, around the big man by a half a step, while bouncing the ball from left hand to right hand, executing the classic crossover. This brought the baseline defender to Jimmy's right forward, which was the next trap set by the zone, and normally would end a foray such as this in the defeat of an awkward shot, or a travel, or a steal. Landing on his right foot, Jimmy was now about ten feet away from the basket, with a six-four guy in his face and the six-six guy he just crossed over leaning alongside him on his left, slightly behind, but with more than enough wingspan to toss away any shot he thought Jimmy could possibly throw up.

Jimmy knew the key to the success of the move was the aggression of the opponent, the utter disdain they would have at someone as skinny and little as he was to have the nerve to take them strong to the hoop with no fear. He jumped off his right foot, with the ball in his right hand, seemingly straight at the right side of the basket. Both defenders jumped as well, angling their bodies to meet Jimmy at the basket and toss his offering into the crowd, but Jimmy had not, in fact, jumped straight at the basket as it seemed. He held the ball out in his right hand to promote the illusion he was leaping straight at the basket to lay it in right handed on the right side of the hoop, an utterly futile maneuver with no chance of success, and the crowd gasped at what was about to be an epic rejection. But the playground trick he had learned so long ago was to jump off the right foot, which when taking a right-handed layup would be the wrong foot, and not leap straight to the basket despite the appearance of doing so. Jumping off his right foot allowed him to push his body ever so slightly to his left, angling it across the lane.

At the same time, the baseline defender on Jimmy's left, the only guy Jimmy was worried about having to influence throughout this whole ballet, wanted to get in on the fun, just as Jimmy hoped he would. He couldn't let the two other big men block a shot he could block himself. Instead of staying at home on Jimmy's left side as he should, he took a step across the basket, so he could be the first to greet Jimmy at the right side of the hoop and hear the cheers from the crowd as he watched the ball he swatted sail into the third row. When Jimmy saw him take the expected fatal step he brought the ball down, in front of his stomach, and changed it into his left hand, while still soaring through the air. Now his left foot was coming down, only a foot off the ground, his left arm was arcing up to release the ball, and not a single of the five guys defending was even on the same side of the rim as the ball as it touched softly against the back board on the left side of the basket and fell without a care through the net. No one had even managed to touch Jimmy. They couldn't have fouled him if they wanted to. Jimmy did a little dance, bouncing around in a circle in three quick hops as the shocked defense looked across and saw how they had been tricked.

The crowd went wild. Despite it being intramurals, a crowd of over one hundred people was there. Basketball in Illinois was taken seriously, at any level. Indiana may have had the best rep, but Illinois had the best players. When it was cold outside, as it was seven or eight months of the year, people congregated in the nearest gym to play or watch, cheering and jeering at the action inside the warm dankness. What they had seen was little Jimmy ducking into a crowd of big strong guys, like a deer running into the forest, and then Jimmy coming out of the opposite end of the crowd untouched, and laying the ball in with a flourish. How he had done it, no one there could fathom as their view was hampered by the thicket of limbs and torsos, but he had no doubt just done it. He had taken a zone to the hole one on five, something any coach worth his salt would say shouldn't even be attempted, scored an easy layup, and no one had laid a hand on him. The TKE fans were screaming as loudly as the Goodfellas fans.

"Hell no, Jimmy!!" called out Sonny Mathis from the crowd.

"Just another J move," answered Jimmy with a shrug as he trotted down the court, and the J was for Dr. J, not Jimmy, as well Sonny knew. Jimmy smiled as he reminisced on all the years of work that went into that move, and realized he had best cherish it, and all the other moves he would make that school year, his last; with the recognition he may never be able to play the sport he so dearly loved with this level of fitness and focus ever again.

Jimmy finished lap eight. The more he focused on breathing deeply, fully, unhurriedly, as he willed each leg forward again and again, the more memories and fantasies floated unimpeded through his mind. His thoughts drifted to his first night on campus as a new student at Bradley, the day for which he had waited for so long. The first day he was finally out of the nest and away from the prying eyes. The first night he was gone from the place that had plagued him for so long with its never-ending sameness. He remembered how the loneliness flooding into him that night was so unexpected, so shocking, in retrospect his reaction to it was not nearly as shocking as it seemed at the time. It was the quiet that did it. In his nest it had never been quiet. There was always music or loud voices or the drone of the television, and usually all three at once. He sat at his cramped desk in his even more cramped dorm room, turned on the light, opened one of the heavy notebooks he had brought with him to take copious notes in his Physics classes and did something he had never conceived of doing before. He wrote the following on the first sheet:

Three Pointers

The sweetness
of a smile,
of a touch,
of one moment – more.
Sophisticated sweetness.
Enrapturing, delightful;
But a touch of class, oh, what a touch!
Shy sweetness.
Self-protecting, soul erecting, re-directing
the sweetness
to a higher plane.
In essence,
the uniqueness is
and will be always
the sweetness.

He counted eleven as the memory of the enchantress who made him spill out such unintelligible words came to his mind. Talia Simone. Never in the eighteen years the universe had been revealing itself to Jimmy had he seen a female with such an astounding figure, with such an effortless way of injecting adrenaline into his veins with a switch of her hips, and such a sweet smile as she turned to watch him watch her do it. On his first day this vision had come to him.

He never gave it to her. Maybe he should have. She would still be nearby, just as shockingly pretty and sweet, mere minutes away in the small, five square block world of the Bradley campus, even though the four years which had passed since he had first met her had not made her any less impossible to approach. Maybe he should have given out all the poems that followed, to all the girls he had written them about, even though Talia had never been replaced as his main muse. Maybe he still could. It wasn't too late. There was one more semester to go.

Deep breaths were in heavy demand for the last three quarters of a mile. The burden of keeping his legs supplied with oxygen had made his lungs burn so hot he needed to breathe with his mouth open wide to cool the inferno roiling in his chest. But he smiled as he thought of how delightful it would feel to make it to the end, and now he was so close he knew he would make it. And he wasn't thinking about the laps still torturing him, he was thinking about the academic journey ending in the coming spring. All that was left for him to complete during his last lap was his Senior Lab course, which was a yearlong effort he and his partner spent the first semester planning and now needed to execute in the second. Their task was to create an analog electronic system which would control the speed of a motor at a constant speed set point regardless of the torque required, using an electronic technique called a phase-locked loop, and they had to do build it from the component level, make it work, then demonstrate it to the faculty at the end of the year. This was cutting edge for Electrical Engineers in 1981.

As this was the early eighties the only people with computers were the nerds Jimmy took classes with who built them from parts bought from Radio Shack. A calculator was considered such a serious purchase Jimmy's dad had driven him alone to the store to buy one, before his freshman year, and made it clear Jimmy had better not break it before he graduated, which if nothing happened between this day and May, he would have obediently accomplished. Jimmy chuckled at that thought, and the fact by this time he was paying for most of his education and had a good paying job offer already in his back pocket. At this point it was about over, and Jimmy had a legacy to think about.

What could he do, besides win the All University Basketball Championship with his intramural team, the Goodfellas, his reason for churning his guts into mush circling the track? He had stopped, having counted to twenty, and was bent over at the waist to suck in air as efficiently as possible. With another two miles under his belt, what could he do indeed? By the time this last break ended he knew he would have to have it figured out.

2. She Took You Where?

Teenagers love more ardently and foolishly than any other creatures on Earth, except male black widow spiders. At that age when you are in love and you think that which you love loves you back, you will go to the most extreme lengths to be together. No warnings or pleading from those who know better will deter you. Those are so easily deflected and crushed like paper airplanes against the solid concrete wall of the teenaged heart wisdom needn't bother to make any futile attempts to penetrate it. And when the teenager is a boy, and his love is for a sport, the wisdom of the universe knows to let it run its course, as it knows the ravages of time and its accompanying debilitating ravages of the tendons will eventually cause the end of the affair.

But when you are fifteen you are so far from ravaged you can't burden your mind imagining its ever occurring. Your love carries you through the cold cruelty of winter and the furnace blasts of summer. When the heat drags on in August you are barely phased and can still love on in the swelter of the blacktop, in air so humid you need to clear a path through it, and breaths with open mouths are sprinkled with flies and gnats to compliment the oxygen. So long as there is a ball and a hoop and others to pass to and steal from, you are one with your love. Even in a barn loft.

Three Pointers

I am no one, I am everyone.
I live to escape instinct.
She was a blond haired, afroed, slanty-eyed, native
And instinct drove me on into the night, searching.
She said, "I've been all around the world.
Where would you like me to show you?"

Escape instinct by creating a technique.
A smile as a recount is taken.
Bending your mind, a squirt in a wet pocket,
A sandy beach, full of futures;
She took you where?

Jimmy wasn't sure why that poem came to his mind, but the memory of the barn was clearly connected to what was happening to him midway through his daily run, three days before he was to return to school. There was a town on Route 9 a few miles outside of Canton named Monterrey, and why someone had felt the need to call it a town was never clear to anyone, as it was just a couple of farm houses and barns on the side of the road. In what would seem strange to a lot of people who think they know what farm people do with their spare time, one of those barns had a loft with a basketball hoop at one end, and an open door policy for anyone to come and play as long as they let the farmer/owner join the game if he was not out in his fields and wasn't too tired. All you had to do was drive out there with a ball, pull off to the side of the road, wave real friendly-like to anyone on the porch of the house or in the yard, go into the barn and carefully sidestep the chickens and their droppings, climb the ladder to the loft, and then strip down to shirts and skins and go at it, except the aforementioned farmer, who always played in his overalls and steel toed shoes.

As with any barn loft, it started at the wall on the long side of the structure and jutted out above the main floor, maybe eight feet, and stretched out about a third of the way across the barn, supported by sturdy wooden poles, and was reached by a thick wooden ladder. After buying a silo the farmer had converted the loft from its original purpose, storing hay, to its current purpose of providing a warm (in spring and fall) and dry slice of hoop heaven by adding a rim at one end and adding first a hand rail, then replacing that with an eight foot high wall made of wood planks on either side of the ladder after tiring of going up and down to retrieve stray passes and bad shots. On the right side of the loft/court, the wall sloped up at a sixty-degree angle, making it impossible to put any of the proper arc on a right baseline jump shot, and in fact, making it possible to get that shot blocked by the wall itself if you were fortunate enough to be that tall or have that much jumping ability. There were of course a few "dead spots", as there were on any wooden floor on which balls were bounced and knowing where they were was an essential part of playing good defense and avoiding embarrassment on offense. And unlike any of the other places Jimmy had found to express his teenaged devotion to his beloved, when he felt the floor boards sink and spring back with each footfall, he knew this could be the day the whole court gave way and the only thing between the players and the hard concrete below was chicken excrement.

August is served thick in central Illinois. It does not come layered with cool dry days. It spreads like a flood of molasses, quickly sticking to everything, its moisture prevalent on the most brilliant of days and the darkest, with either the clouds pouring it out in big hard drops or the people sweating it out in the humidity of the sun. On so many days rain is flung down with absolute fury until it is chased away by a blazing burst of sun which is then as quickly splashed away by another bank of dark rogues in the sky, it is as if the gods cannot decide which way to best punish the young lovers for their audacity, but if they be so bold as to climb a ladder they can still escape.

And that is why instead of moping about the puddles on all the nearby blacktop, about the locks on all the doors of the gyms, and about the backyard court recently declared off-limits by the new owners of the house in front of it; six besotted boys, wearing sweatbands and tight shorts and canvas shoes with rips and holes in them, squished into a car driven by the only one old enough to drive one legally, and journeyed to Monterrey to play out their passions. Waiting for tomorrow or some other day when the clouds were not so bountiful and the air not so thick was not even considered. Jimmy was squeezed into the middle of the front seat, with the driver, Bob Bortolini, on one side and his younger brother Bennie on the other, and Donny Demoss, Sonny Mathis, and Greg Hart shoulder to shoulder in the back. Even with all the windows rolled down the heat was oppressive, but that was like a dip in a mountain stream compared to the conditions in the loft. All had water rolling down their backs by the time they climbed into the steam room and began to play.

The game they used to loosen up was called, in polite circles, "Twenty-One", and in the impolite circles these boys travelled in was called "Fight". It was quite simple. One ball, one hoop, and every man for himself. The game began when the ball was placed on the ground, at the free throw line if there was one, and the players circled around it. Someone said "go" and there was a scramble for the ball, and whoever snatched it had to plow, fake, or quick his way to the basket, or to any kind of open shot he could get, and if the shot was made, he tallied 2 points and was given the right to take 3 free throws maximum. He had to make the first to get the second, and the second to get the third. If he made all three he was given the ball at the top of the key to try to score again. When a shot was missed whoever won the rebound could go straight up with it, take it out for a jump shot, or do whatever they needed to try to score. When the first player reached seven points, all the players who still had zero were eliminated, and the guys still left standing fought it out until the winner reached 21 points.

That meant the best strategy was to try to score seven straight points if you scored first, and if that didn't work to try to prevent those who still hadn't scored from scoring until someone reached seven, while at the same time trying to stay as much as possible under the basket to rebound someone else's miss. If you still had zero points it was in your best interest to make sure someone with 5 points didn't score again, so you had to play brutal defense if that person got the ball. If six guys were playing, the result was one guy had the ball, and two or three would guard him, and two or three would be under the basket fighting for position. Aggression, toughness, and quick thinking and decision making were the keys to this game, and, also, if you could make your free throws you could keep elbows out of your face at least some of the time. The difference between "Twenty-One" and "Fight" was the normal rules of basketball applied to Twenty-One, and the only rule of Fight was there were no rules. That meant no fouls, travelling, double dribbles, etc. could be called, and if anyone complained about being roughed up, they were sent home to watch soap operas with their sisters.

As Jimmy was the smallest and weakest of the six players, this was not a game in which he could hope to excel, but it was a joy for him none the less. Geometry and physics rule any activity involving mass, space, and time, and to Jimmy basketball was the purest way to use his knowledge of both to grant him license to be endlessly and aggressively creative. Because he could not stop the bigger boys from knocking him down and pushing him aside if he tried to position himself under the basket, he learned to stand out of the reach of their arms and watch the arc of shots and determine which way they would bounce off the iron, so he could arrive where the ball would carom before any of his competitors, and dash in and leap to tip it in or grab it before they could stop him. He learned to throw the ball against the backboard instead of trying to shoot it straight in when they did grab him and were tossing him to the ground. He learned to not wait until a bigger guy backed him down and used his bulk to move him out of the way to get off a shot, but to rob him of the ball as soon as he touched it, to find the angle from which the ball would come and use his delicate fingers to not clutch it, but to tip it somewhere safe where only he could get it. He learned despite all the best timing and quick thinking he could muster, sometimes the only reward for his effort was a fat lip. And most importantly, he learned the tricks of shooting quickly, that the basket was fixed in space and it was he who was moving relative to it, so he should always know where it was and not need to locate it until the point of release, in fact he should be able to shoot blindfolded.

He had to be able to shoot while he was jumping up, at the peak of his jump, on the way down, or standing still. He had to be able to shoot knowing he was going to land on his back. And most of all, he had to believe it was going in when he shot it, no matter the angle or under what pile of duress he was buried, that it was best for him to expect to be off-balance when he released the ball, and be able to make the necessary corrections with his wrist and fingers, and to be sure to rejoice in those rarities of a balanced unencumbered look at the basket and take advantage with a textbook, confident stroke. In other words, to make his free throws, because it hurt a lot less when he did.

That game taught him so many things. On this day he learned the beauty of the left baseline jumper. It all started with a scrum under the basket. The Bortolini boys had smashed together and with Donny Demoss in mid-air chasing a misfire by Greg, caused by Sonny grabbing his left arm when he jumped for the shot, forcing Greg to throw the ball hard against the backboard instead of shooting it. When it clanged against the front of the rim and bounced straight up, the three boys timed their jumps and synchronized their collision. The brothers cancelled each other out and Donny was the only one able to reach up and swat at the ball, even though he could not grab it as he was forced by the mass of Bortolini crashing into him away from where the ball was coming down.

The ball arced away from them, and Jimmy, standing outside the vortex of fury under the basket, saw it angling for the left corner of the court, along the baseline. He knew Sonny and Greg had seen it too, and would be racing for the same spot, but also knew he would arrive a fraction of a second before them. Then he would have to catch it, turn quickly, line up his elbow, and flick his wrist all in one motion, or they would be on him and wrestle it away before he could shoot it.

And so, he did, and his love responded, as it had so many times in this long rapture of devotion. The ball leaving his hands felt like the sun rising in the east in the morning, as it rose it knew exactly where to go and there was no doubt where it would set. He watched as it rotated, climbing into the thick air, but then the beauty of its flight was blanked out by the bodies covering him, a thick forearm trying its best to dislodge the air from his chest, and all he could see were rafters and cobwebs.

Surprisingly he could still breathe when the pile of Sonny and Greg unfolded and uncovered him, and by the fact Donny was holding the ball with a look of disgust on his face, he knew the shot had gone in. After making his first free throw, he missed the second, and once again the ball was batted into the same corner. Somehow no one else saw where it was going, and Jimmy was gifted with being able to watch his next corner jumper as it arced so beautifully and precisely through the rim the others vowed it would be his last. Despite this, before they left the loft that day Jimmy knew no matter if he was off-balance, falling out of bounds backwards or to the side, had a hand in his face or an elbow in his stomach, once he found the range on the baseline jumper it was harder to miss one than make one, even with his eyes closed. The others made sure at least one of those was occurring, and sometimes more than one, on every shot he tried again. By the time they were ready to call it quits and go home for their other favorite pastime, eating dinner, he had made one with his eyes closed just to show off.

That was why when he was stopped after lap 9 that day and ordered to leave the Y he could smile. It wasn't so harsh. In a couple more days he would be leaving anyway, and going back to the place in which he had made so many memories and still had a few more to make in the one last semester he had to make them in. His college cup, whether full or not, was about to be taken from him, and he was humble and wise enough to rejoice in how far he had been allowed to run and not worry about the distance yet to be traversed. As it had happened so many times before in his journey of love, he expected a new blessing around each blind corner of every detour, a new skill to be uncovered each time he was made to suffer, and when he came upon a raging lion or an angry mob, the clarity to use that blessing or skill to overcome.

3. Third Unrelated Thought on the Same Thing

He left at night, under cover of darkness, as if he was afraid the authorities of Canton would be watching during the day and not allow him to go, knowing if they didn't stop him this time he may never be back again. He chuckled to himself. They would probably give him a free tank of gas if they knew this was it, and he was leaving his small-town existence behind forever, so they could be sure he got as far away as they could help him get.

Even in the pitch black of a starless night he could feel the signposts of his life as he passed them on his trip down Route 9. Scott Michaels' house, just a quarter mile from the city limits, where he had ridden a horse for the first time. The farm road on the opposite side a couple of miles further down, where his brother's car had been trapped in mud after returning from fishing in a farmer's pond. Monterrey, coming and going in a flash after the first big turn, five miles out of town, the barns and houses covered in snow. Winding down the hill to the 24 Junction and the hamlet of Banner, with its infamous motel and adjoining liquor store. Gliding along the pavement of Route 24, mimicking the curves of the river all the way to Bartonville, with thoughts of Thanksgivings past and the anticipation of the feast to come on the way to Grandma's house, nestled with his siblings in the back seat of his father's Oldsmobile. Sneaking past the pizza parlor parking lot where he crashed Sonny's Caddy when they were seniors in high school and entering the city limits of Peoria on Adams Street, secure in the knowledge even this town couldn't contain him, he had bigger places to go and conquer. Making the left down Western, a few blocks away from the big white house on the corner that had held the yearly feast, now falling into disrepair in the deteriorating ghetto. Up the hill to the campus, covered with trees barren in the winter chill, and ivy shorn of its leaves clinging to the old brick buildings to absorb whatever heat and comfort it could extract.

After dropping his bags and greeting his roommate, there was only one place to go, Haussler Hall, the campus gymnasium. The people he expected to be there were there; Hal Green and Tyrone Bowers, the starting forwards on the Goodfellas, along with all the other gym rats who spent time at Haussler on most of the good-weather days and all the bad-weather days on campus; and even some he hadn't, like Darrell Everett their center. Maybe it was the cold, or the anticipation tinged with dread caused by the reality of another semester's worth of lectures and exams being upon them - starting for some as early as 8 AM the next morning - or the overwhelming fondness the long month of absence had infused in those who had been separated for too long from a distant lover, but the air was filled with the euphoria of old boys spliced into young men shouting and running with glee, like toddlers let loose on the playground after a morning filled with A-B-C's in the warmth of spring.

"Jimmy! Wassup?" shouted Hal as he bounded across the court to greet his teammate. As always, he was smiling through his tightly maintained moustache and goatee, his long arms dangling down the sides of his six-foot, three-inch frame, his long delicate fingers matched with even longer legs. True to his natural talent as a slasher, he slipped his way through the twisted mass of humanity chasing balls and dashing around him, and stopped in front of his friend without making any contact.

"You, man," responded Jimmy as they slapped each other's hands. "I hope you guys've been stayin' in shape and not just eatin," he teased.

He said "guys" in plural because trotting up behind Hal, in his normal methodical style, not caring if he stepped into the path of the others milling around him, was Tyrone.

"Naw, man, just eatin," chuckled Tyrone, holding his stomach with both hands.

Tyrone was a little above six-four and had one hundred eighty-five pounds chiseled onto his long, strong, frame, and at this point in his young life heavy meals slid off him without leaving much of a trace. That in combination with his light skin and wavy hair made him the type girls went weak for; and his strong physique, bolstered by years in the weight room, made him the type who could hold his position under the basket and force others to go around him, like water around a boulder in the middle of a churning torrent.

"Well, I've been runnin' two miles a day," said Jimmy, staring hard at the pair.

Tyrone returned his smaller friend's stare and admitted, "I couldn't run that far in a month."

Hal chimed in, "What's the matter, you couldn't go hoopin' with the 82nd Airborne like last year?"

"Naw," said Jimmy, "That was once in a lifetime."

If you've given your heart, your soul, your entire ego to your love, there is no force between heaven and hell that can deter you from proclaiming it with all the fervor your spirit contains to whatever uncaring or unbelieving audience is in front of you; and if that love is true and pure those who mock you will be transformed by its boldness. The odds stacked against you will crumble at your feet.

He hadn't gone to North Carolina to stand in judgment, to be mocked and scorned, to be held accountable for what those staring down at him saw as pure folly at best or injuriously dangerous at worst. He had come to visit his older brother for Christmas, stationed at Fort Bragg, home of the 82nd Airborne, the Army division filled with testosterone oozing young men trained to jump out of perfectly good airplanes and kill whatever moved once they hit the ground. But it was of no surprise when his brother insisted they go to their gym on a Saturday afternoon, when the best players congregated to show off their dominance at the place where all their friends could watch, and he was standing at center court surrounded by nine others whose only job was to build their bodies and hone their aggression while he spent those same hours staring at books full of formulas and abstract ideas. They were laughing at his skinny legs and arms, every man in the stands and on the court knowing they could snap them in multiple ways within ten seconds, and at the chest they knew would reveal each rib bone with his shirt removed, and the innocence and fear splashed across his face as he stared at the multitudes with tears in their eyes in anticipation of the comedic entertainment about to occur.

Then the game began. As he was the smallest guy on the court, his inclusion in the game only assured after his brother and a friend went toe to toe with the biggest ugliest soldier in the gym, he was tasked with playing point guard, bringing the ball up court and passing it to the bigger guys, to catcalls and shouts of derision as he dribbled his way across the half court line. The fear on his face was very real, and his nervousness made him want to get the ball out of his hands as quickly as possible, but true love is always stronger than feelings of weakness, and when no one aggressively picked him up after he was a couple of dribbles into the front court he realized he must react to what in his mind was a sign of serious disrespect, that he could not possibly love the way he knew how to love , and his spirit demanded he punish the non-believers immediately by pulling up at the wing extended and letting loose with a love letter concealed in a jump shot anyone watching would know as pure.

As he watched the ball rising and rotating, the spin perfect, the arc of the shot in synchronicity with the gravity controlling it, he knew it was going to splash through the net without touching the rim and didn't bother tracking it to its inevitable conclusion. He wanted those who doubted him to know he had none, so he watched them instead as he slowly backpedaled down the court to play defense.

"Damn!!" shouted someone who was watching him watch them, "He's goin' down court like he knows it's gonna fall!!"

That's when the ball stretched the cords as it dropped through, and all the eyes that had been watching its flight turned to the skinny kid standing alone at the opposite end of the court, and the voices filled with laughter seconds before were now cheering. But not for long. As soon as the ball touched the ground and was picked up by the opposing team, it was in-bounded. The big dude who objected so strongly to Jimmy's participation had drifted to half court to start a fast break since he didn't think the shot would fall, and the ball was speeding toward him in a flash. As he had looked over at Jimmy when everyone else did, he did not see the pass as it was launched. When Jimmy realized he didn't see it coming, his creativity came to the fore and he sprinted at full speed straight at the big man, with his fists balled, shouting at him at the top of his lungs like he was attacking him in a fit of rage.

"What choo doin'??" the big man screamed as he watched the skinny pipsqueak launch himself. In disbelief he too balled his fists, wondering what kind of martial art or madness was contained inside the little man rushing toward him.

"He's rippin' you!!!!" shouted the loud mouth in the stands as he realized Jimmy's intent, and sure enough, one stride away from his opponent, Jimmy stepped in front of him and reached out and caught the pass the big man had still not realized was a few feet away.

The laughter that followed energized both Jimmy and his opponent, so much so that both raced down the court, Jimmy dribbling straight to the basket with the big man hot on his heels, a nasty reunion awaiting him if he was so foolish as to try to take the ball all the way to the cup, something no one in the gym thought he would be insane enough to do, seeing the other four players standing there waiting for him, flexing biceps bigger than his thighs and menacingly evil smiles on their faces. But true love provides the devoted with such creative soil new life can spring forth in the most unexpected places, through minuscule cracks in the concrete, and Jimmy jumped straight at the basket anyway. He reinforced the collective disbelief in the gym by glancing at a teammate and pushing the ball away from his chest as if to pass, which was the only outcome they could believe. No one matched his jump to stop what they could not process was unfolding, an easy, uncontested layup. Love knows no limitations.

Three Pointers

When she kissed him,
She watched as he rolled back his eyes…

Nice take.
Came down the lane with a shake and bake,
Decided to float, then dish left,
High five to the other end.

Pick up near the hash, slide down the side
Through traffic, quick cut in the middle
Off to the wing, pressure from inside
Fight through, look up at the pass
One quick step, and sky, and turn, and watch it fall.

Shoot eyes in direction of feet and hands up for the break,
Remarkably smooth transition, in setting up the wing pops,
Swing it his way, escape to the cup
Moment's hesitation causes go-end to be aborted.
Circle up baseline left, see D, and slide to the side to
See it go to the open man, shoot to half
O board and drift to the key, set for maximum smooth, release.

"So, gentlemen," said Jimmy with more than a hint of sarcasm, "You know this is my last chance."

His friends chuckled at the seriousness of his tone. Daryl had quietly joined their circle, as timid as he was large, and at six foot six and tipping the scale above two hundred it was hard to be timid, but he managed it on most nights and in most games.

"The All-U's?" responded Hal. "There ain't no team out there that can stop us from winnin' it this year."

"Yeah, you're right," shot back Jimmy. "But we can stop us. Especially if we're draggin' in the last five minutes."

"Then we'll just have to blow everyone out," said Tyrone, as if that was as easy to do as it was obvious.

"Man, you know we don't blow people out. We win ugly, with our defense," corrected Jimmy, "And we need to be in shape for that."

His teammates nodded in agreement, and then Hal smiled and said, "Well, we won't get in any shape standin' here talkin'. Let's get in some run before the night's over."

And so they did, huffing and puffing until the lights were turned out.

4. Senior Phase

Papichulo was a unique figure on Bradley's campus, so unique he could join all the cliques he desired, so popular he was endowed with automatic access into every sorority house after dark. Even the notoriously snooty Pi Phi house, filled with immaculate blonds, flush with their fathers' credit cards and cars at their disposal, had him on their entry list. And when he felt like slumming it, he could breeze into the basement toga parties held off campus by the Q's, the basest clan of brothers on The Yard. Being from Panama was the ice-breaker, speaking Spanish and English with a funny accent to either group of native speakers - not that there were any native Spanish speakers in this bland neck of the Midwest - and he had learned being from a foreign land made his blackness palatable to the lighter skinned, and acceptable to the darker. Being gregarious by nature was the key that unlocked all doors; and his size - a muscular six three topped with a three-inch Afro - and ready smile disarmed all those within.

Jimmy met Papichulo in their freshman year like most people met Papichulo, when Papichulo walked up to him and stuck out his hand as if they were sure to be the best of friends. That hadn't happened, but since they were both studying Electrical Engineering, they became acquaintances to a closer and closer degree as their group of co-students shrank from one hundred in their first semester of study to fifty in their last. Papichulo's journey of discovery of American culture had forced him to understand some would not accept him despite all his efforts, and the underlying principles which led to that conclusion were now obvious to him. He wasn't black enough for some and was far too black for even more. He refused to align himself with any camp if it required the exclusion of others, which resulted in him walking alone with his head held high as he traversed this strange culture's minefields.

It was Papichulo who suggested before the summer break they be lab partners for this most important class of all, their Senior Lab. Actually, he insisted on it, with quite the air of the decision having been made already, stating they must prove to the rest of the forty eight taking this last class with them the two darkest members of the exclusive club they had labored in for four years could do the work and make the required demonstration and presentation without the crutch of a straight haired partner. Jimmy had accepted with relief, having no desire to deal with the skepticism that lingered amongst some of his colleagues - someone had to be taking his tests for him, he was graded on a more lenient curve, he had been given more help and support than they from a faculty needing to have at least one minority graduate - despite the fact they had seen him in most if not all of their classes giving accurate answers and asking probing questions.

"So, what's eet going to be, Jeemmy?" asked Papichulo as they sat together at their lab table on the first day of class. He may have been the most outgoing personally, but he knew who should be making the technical decisions between the two of them.

"We're going to design a phase locked loop," said Jimmy with all the confidence his years of academic excellence had brought him. He did not love what he was doing, whether he realized it at this stage of his life or not, but he could do it and make a good living at it, he was sure.

"A what?" asked Papichulo, needing some clarification.

"The latest electronic way to control the speed of a motor," replied Jimmy impatiently. "We have to build a circuit to read the speed then feed it back to another circuit that outputs a control signal to the motor to speed it up or slow it down. To make it easier we'll use a motor that needs to run at a constant speed then come up with some way to load it and unload it to vary the torque required, so our loop will have to react in a way to keep it from slowing down or speeding up. You know, the way the turn table on a record player needs to work."

"OK, sure," replied Papichulo with an air of complete confidence at the same time as an air of doubt. "You write up the proposal and give it to me and I'll polish it up," he said, and with that they parted ways, Jimmy to dash off to the gym and Papichulo to saunter over to sorority row.

Out on the Illinois prairie
A man can be as free
As his responsibilities.

Tenderness is as fleeting as
A feather floating upon a storm,
Wind etched life revealing clear cut realities,
Entered as a continuum of doors.

After it all I cry,
For my verse will be read in shadow,
And my tears flow in the light.

When you've taken all from someone
All you can return is love,
Even you are not a lost cause
And they will return if there's something you've forgotten.

So you want a free ticket?
Time tells on the victim of entertainment
Always at your own expense.
Sometimes the fiddler demands payment in blood —
Of any type.

Those who know you inside and out
Can never know what's inside your mind —
The motivation inside the motivation,
The caricature of a rhyme.

When the tree falls,
And the night calls,
Onward and upward in the land of smiles —
Any room for a late arrival?

That day seemed so long ago for Jimmy, even though it occurred only a few months before. So much work had been done, and so much more was still needed. So much had happened in his life before arriving at this juncture it was hard to comprehend it was narrowing down to this point so soon, and yet after so many classes and courses of study, Senior Lab was all that was left before passing over into adulthood. There had been so many close calls.

Chicago was a hoopster's paradise. Every playground held the promise of nirvana. There was no guarantee of greatness there, only a guarantee of competition, and that was enough to keep the courts full of life whether the sun shone brightly in blue skies or dimly behind clouds before they released waves of wetness onto the asphalt. Jimmy spent every dry weekend on one court or another during the summer of 1979. He had landed a summer job at American Oil Company, working as a nicely paid intern for the company that would employ him as soon as he removed his cap and gown in the spring of 1981. One of his best friends from college, Eddie Morris, asked him to come to his house and go to his neighborhood blacktop a block away, which was one of the most extreme compliments a guy could get. If you brought a friend to play in front of your homies he had better be good or your street cred would be diminished indirectly by his ineptitude, and in neighborhoods like this street cred was sometimes all that kept you alive.

By this time Jimmy knew the deal, and when the activities began with a game of Twenty-One, not Fight, he knew he had to show all his wares. With so many guys in such a small space, the best way to get it going was to take the ball as far as his range would allow, and rise and release a jump shot to show the technical skill he had been taught and been practicing since the fifth grade. To correctly shoot a jump shot means to start with your feet hip width apart, with your big toes pointed straight at the target, the rim. Everything, from your feet to your knees to your heart beating in your chest to your nose and eyes should be in line with the rim. The ball should be held in your hands with the fingers of your favored hand placed along one of the seams, and your opposite hand placed on the side of the ball with your palm centered where the seams meet. The motion starts with a deep bend in your knees with your back straight, such that your ankles bend to keep you from falling and to coil your spring. The jump begins with your feet, the heels rising first, then the balls of your feet pushing away from the ground as your calves and thighs flex in unison to launch your body away from the Earth. As you rise your favored arm should be bent at a ninety-degree angle, its elbow pointed straight toward the basket, your wrist bent at the same angle such that the palm of the hand is facing skyward and heel of the hand is facing the target. As you become airborne you must raise your arm at the shoulder, keeping the elbow and wrist bent and when you reach the top of your jump smoothly straighten the elbow, and with a harmonious flow only possible after many hours of repetition, uncoil your wrist with a flick such that the ball rolls down the fingers and leaves the tip of your middle finger last. Your arm must remain pointed toward the goal exactly, without the elbow bending outward or inward, to make your aim true. The flick of the wrist is what gives the ball the proper rotation, its beautiful arc, and allows it to land softly when it is slightly off-course and meets the rim instead of splashing directly through, increasing the odds that it then falls in and does not bounce away, what is aptly described as a "shooter's touch". It is as hard to describe as it is easy to see when it is done properly.

And the shooter must be so well practiced he does not think of any of this as he rises, he must only think, as Jimmy shouted as it left his hands, "That's goin' in!"

Same technique on his free throws, except instead of pushing himself off the ground with his legs, he pushed himself with the least amount of force required to inject enough momentum into his torso to straighten his arm and release the ball. The trick with free throws is to use the same pre-shot routine, to allow your muscles to remember exactly what the least amount of force should be. Jimmy's was to first grab his triple layered socks with each hand, to dry whatever sweat had dripped onto them, by bending at the waist before he received the ball, and then dry his forehead with a wrist band. Next, he took the ball and dribbled it once, twice, and then a third time, while shifting his weight from one hip to the other and catching it each time with both hands instead of one; then he lined up the fingers of his left hand along one of the curved seams, never one of the straight ones. He bent his knees much deeper than on a jump shot, and slowly rose keeping his feet flat, all to put just enough energy into his release and never too much. The arm motion was the same, the flick of the wrist the same, the rotation of the ball the same. All with the intent to deliver the ball to the rim with its momentum totally consumed, with no energy left to allow it to carom away, for it to drop with a soft sigh through the cords of the net.

One, then two, then three free throws fell, and when he was tossed the ball with a chance to shutout all competitors without anyone else getting off a shot, he was surrounded and hounded and pushed so far away that his efforts at a shutout were shutout instead. The ball scared the rim at least, managing to strike it hard and low with no chance of bouncing up and into it, and a scramble ensued which resulted in a rebound, a missed bank shot, a swat at a tip in, and then finally an attempt that hesitated and rolled around the iron before falling in by one of the many contenders battling under the basket. Before he managed to get close to the basket again four others had scored, both Eddie and his younger brother Evan among them.

As Evan stood at the line and shot his first free throw, Jimmy saw it was off to the left and made his leap as the ball bounced high along the left baseline, his favorite place to make a falling fade away as he had done so many times before. He gathered in the ball, reaching his long arms over the outstretched hands of one of the shorter boys straining to get his first chance to score, but when he turned to take the shot he had such confidence in, Eddie, taller and longer and cognizant of what was on Jimmy's mind, stepped close and took that option away.

One of the beauties of basketball is when circumstances force you away from your plan creativity can replace it with something far grander. Instead of taking the jump shot his friend saw coming and would alter with a wave of his hand, Jimmy pump faked. As Eddie rose from his feet to take on the challenge, Jimmy instead dropped the ball to the ground and took a big step with his right leg and let the ball rise into his left hand. The baseline was left uncovered, and Jimmy had the instantaneous vision of the move he had to try to make, to honor his hero and mentor, the incomparable Julius Erving. Bending his knee for maximum lift, he sprung from the asphalt to make it appear he was going strong to the left side of the rim for a lay in, causing the crowd around the basket to leap in unison in response, to meet the ball as it travelled toward the backboard and snuff it out. This was the vision Jimmy wanted them to have, and when they had left the ground on their mission of destruction he brought the ball down and held it in both hands in front of his waist, using the physical law of action and reaction to allow his torso to travel farther than it would otherwise before his feet returned to the ground, just far enough to extend his left arm with his wrist bent to cup the ball to the right side of the rim. As if in slow motion, all the hands attached to arms long enough to touch the backboard smacked against the left side of it, searching for a ball that was not there, and the ball arced silently, like a cat burglar through a moon lit window, up and over the right side of the rim and down through the cords.

"Hah!!" cried Jimmy as the others watched in horror, shock, and dismay and called out "I thought you saw that coming!!" to his friends.

"Seeing it coming and stopping it are two different things," responded Evan, owner of one of the hands misplaced on the wrong side of the rim.

"There was just too much move," said Eddie with admiration.

They were not in the minority, as far as being admirers of a move that to aficionados was about sixty percent of what Julius had done to the Lakers in the Finals a few years prior. Accomplishing any move containing over half of what the master had shown was possible was enough to stick in the memories of mere mortals such as the assembled throng.

"Too bad it was a foul!!" called out the boy who had been robbed of the ball to start it all.

When the crowd laughed and did not console him or give license to his officiating, he stormed off the court, past the trees lining it, and stomped furiously across the half block of the park, not wishing to watch the remainder of the struggle which was now reduced from the twenty it had started with to the five left standing.

They had gone on to a game of five on five, full court, when he returned silently. All the boys had forgotten his tantrum amongst the flurry of activity that followed; others had been fouled, robbed, and had their shots rejected or inexplicably roll off the rim without any great anger erupting, despite the many disputes over fouls, double dribbles and traveling which accompany any pick-up game. Players who want to play more than argue get over these slights and play on, even though there are always a few competing for the title of Mindy Rudolph of the Blacktop.

The anger he held onto so tightly would not be contained long enough for him to move past the trees before he pulled the gun from his waistband and began shooting, much to the shock of most and to the chagrin of the few who had seen it before. He had no real target, and even less aim, as his rage was what was in control, but random bullets can kill just as easily as those fired with calm intent, and the boys scattered in all directions same as the projectiles.

Jimmy hated to run. It brought him much more pain than pleasure, and because of his desire to avoid it as much as possible he had been proven as one of the slowest runners whenever a group of boys contested it. There had been one such contest the year before where Evan had proven he was faster than most, and had left Jimmy in his wake without much effort. But on this day, he was straining, breathing hard in his attempt to keep contact with Jimmy, as Jimmy's strides were as long as he hoped his life would be. In his mind he was outrunning the bullets, as futile as Physics had taught that was, and he refused to slow down despite that fact. Three blocks later he finally yielded to his friend's gasping demands he slow down and came to a stop at the corner of 101st and Lowe.

5. Found a Job

Let me see/hear,
First off, I'd figure out what a 'counterpoise' was,
Then straight to "we obviously conclude…", etc.

Mellow tone,
Microphone,
Sweet voice whispered on the phone,
No time, no time
To be alone.

Have you ever looked up
From gut level,
Felt your gaze level with the horizon,
Between a double rainbow,
Inside the echo of a storm,
And concluded your manhood must prevail?

Touch and go.
Don't leave none of your shit on the bedroom floor,
And step out into the stained society
(Once out there)
Shapes,
In a very ancient part of my brain,
Stain – and I can't complain.
(Twice coming back)
Stay and play,
Itemize as a carefree day.

Oh, by the way,
Somebody said you can't write like jazz,
You gotta write like a skinny kid, from Canton.

Whou the phone rang Jimmy thankfully latched onto the receiver like a life-preserver, his head was drowning in the problem he was trying to solve. Not the answer to the problem, but what the problem itself meant. The answer may not be so difficult, but he was clueless as to what was being asked, so at this point an answer was impossible. He wrote the poem to swim his way out.

That was why he had to chuckle when the man on the other end said, "I am calling to offer you a job when you graduate in May, and I am confident you will not get a better offer than this one. That's why I am calling you so early, so you can have it in your mind as other offers come through. No one will match this offer, I can assure you. I'll send it to you formally by mail, but I can give you the number now."

Then he paused for affect. "Twenty-four thousand, three hundred per year."

Jimmy hadn't said a word since confirming the man was speaking to the person he was trying to contact. He still did not speak. This was a big number. He was thinking of his father, who owned a house, two cars, had five children and had two presently in college to support, and did not make this much money. He was about to be rich beyond his former expectation. Anything over twenty grand would be acceptable to his classmates, as that target had been discussed amongst them many times. Only those planning to work for their fathers were expecting more. Most would happily settle for eighteen. Twenty-four grand was twenty percent more than the target, his mathematically trained brain calculated in a flash. That was more than two grand a month!!

But first he had to decipher what a counterpoise was, to solve the problem he was faced with, or he wouldn't be graduating in the spring to collect those huge, seemingly mythical paychecks. He had to laugh at the thought.

"That's funny?" asked the now nervously panting man, wondering if the kid on the other end of the line already had a better offer, and was therefore not impressed.

"No, sir," said Jimmy, now more worried about the perceived offense than his recently perceived notion of the improbability of reaching the required milestone. "It is a very generous offer. Thank you."

In later years he would learn his first response had been the perfect one for negotiating purposes. He might have cleared the 25K barrier if he had kept up the nonchalance and not succumbed so easily. But for now negotiating even at this level was beyond him, and the only response possible was, "I'm sure it will be the best offer I get, and I look forward to working with American this spring."

"Great!" responded the man on the other end, his confidence brimming. He had closed the deal and could relax and move on to his next task. "I'll let you get on with your studying. Look for the letter. It should arrive in the next few days."

"OK," agreed the still startled Jimmy, but as soon as he dropped the receiver he returned to the same dilemma he was mired in before the phone rang. What the hell was a counterpoise? The math path that followed would be easy, but without a place to start, no formula could guide him. Maybe it was just a ruse, as the level of problems he was now tasked with usually came spiked with useless information to obscure the real issue; the math no longer the main theme, the ability to think critically being what was on trial.

The difference between work and love is work is filled with stressful roadblocks, and love is filled with creative challenges, things to look forward to instead of dread. Like the second day Jimmy went to Haussler Hall, after proving to all on the first day he could not be left alone on the baseline, was a sharp shooter from the wing extended, and was dangerous from anywhere in the semi-circle band of the court fifteen to eighteen feet from the backboard. They had all seen enough of his stroke to know it was not luck causing those shots to fall. So the word was out, and on this day whenever the ball was in his hands from that range his opponents would crowd him, put their hands in his face, and apply the pressure they knew would not allow him to rise and let fly in the rhythm a shooter thrives on.

After a couple of meek passes to thwart their intentions his love could no longer be stifled. Since they wanted to come between him and his lover he would have to formulate some other way. The next pass received was followed by an exaggerated head and shoulder fake, to draw in what he expected, followed by a quick step and dribble down the baseline, and to the shock of his defenders, an easy layup. All the size and jumping ability around him was not enough. The next opportunity, from the top of the key, was a result of the lesson recently learned, and Jimmy made a left then a right fake before bouncing the ball ahead of himself down the lane and rising off his right leg leading to a soft semi-hook over the outstretched arms surrounding him. Then it was on to the next move, and the next, disdaining wide open jump shots in favor of the overflowing baubles in his newly found toy chest, and before his second day in the gym was over he found no one quicker who could jump with him, and no leaper who could fathom his next move and rise in time to stop him. If they had not been so intent on stifling him from the outside, and he had not been so full of love, he would never have been so bold as to attempt what was now his to exploit.

In the end his roommate supplied the definition. As a civil engineer in the making, this was a word, a concept he was well versed in.

"A counterpoise is a weight that balances another weight," explained Roy, after Jimmy struggled with his memories for an hour before he walked in the room.

"A what that does what?" asked Jimmy, wondering why Roy was talking in riddles instead of clear language.

"You know, like the penny you put on the record needle, to keep it from skipping," he replied.

Ahhhh, back to that analogy again, thought Jimmy. Everything was coming back to his main task, the Senior Lab experiment. With that clue in his palm, along with his mechanical pencil, the math flowed from his brain, down his neck, through his arm and into his fingers and half an hour and a page and a half of scribbles later it was solved, and he put on his shorts and sneakers and headed off for another tryst at Haussler.

6. Seventeen New Positions #2

"Do clothes make the man?" probed Dr. Pickard in his fine British accent. He had written down this same question on the blackboard once his cherished group of seniors had entered the classroom, but he repeated it verbally, to make sure they had read it and it had sunk in. He was from the old school even by the conservative standards of Bradley and was the most venerated and titled member of an esteemed faculty. He had been the one most upset when the time-tested requirement for freshman engineers since antiquity - learning the use of the Slide Rule - was abandoned only two years before they had begun their college careers. His dignity would not, however, permit him to change his teaching style and allow the students to read from a textbook. Every lecture was hand written on the chalkboard as he doled out the theories and formulas of electrical physics and the learners were forced to copy each word into their notebooks, or they wouldn't have any study materials. If they were too sick or hung over or busy cramming for a test in another class to attend on any given day they needed to have a good friend whose handwriting was legible, or their grade point average was in immediate jeopardy.

This was Senior Ethics class, a course Dr. Pickard not only championed but in fact was the lone faculty member to see any value in, and the one he took the most pride in teaching. He wanted to ensure none of his students upon leaving the ivy-covered walls and tree lined avenues of academia blindly used the training he had given them over the span of the last four years to destroy the world, to further its demise, to think of technology as an omnipotent god to be worshipped without question, to believe progress equaled morality.

"I'm an engineer!!" blurted one of the believers, Cory Black, without thinking any further. That statement alone was enough to close the subject in his mind. Engineers, everyone knows, do not allow themselves to be buffeted by the winds of fashion. Cory was the type who knew exactly how engineers should act and think and knew the script to follow, so this class was a complete waste of his time. His was the majority opinion, as most of those around him believed with absolute conviction this was the most unproductive hour per week they would have to endure during their matriculation, a step below the 100 level English and Art Appreciation classes they had worn their molars down on in their freshman year.

"Is that why you have a pocket protector in your shirt?" asked one of his classmates, to get the laugh he was duly rewarded by the rest of the group. Frank Torrez was constantly making dry comments like this. He was never anything but cool, except on the day the discussion of the merits of minorities receiving preferential admissions was brought forth. He was strongly against it even though his real name being Francisco and his last name being Torrez had vaulted him above many others when it came time to pick the lucky few who were admitted to Bradley without having a parent rich enough to buy their entry. He had made it clear he was NOT Hispanic, he just had a Hispanic name, and his white skin and lack of an accent should be enough to keep him from being forced to wear that label.

Before his target could think of an answer, Dr. Pickard asked a more pointed question. "Aren't those new pants you are wearing? What was wrong with the old ones?"

Since Cory was thoroughly convinced he had all the answers to any questions raised in an Ethics class, he didn't need to think before he made his response. "The old ones were getting shiny!"

When the rest of the class stopped laughing, because his new pants, and he always wore corduroys, never blue jeans, were as equally ridiculous looking as his old ones, Jimmy cried out, "If you don't care about clothes, what difference does that make?"

"I'm not walking around with shiny pants!" shot back Cory, the look on his face telling the world it should be obvious why he bought new pants.

"So you do care about clothes," was the measured response of Ian Dickenson in his superior British accent, as if he was Sherlock Holmes having uncovered the murderer. Ian was the only one in the class who was planning, and was assuredly on the path to acceptance, to continue his engineering studies in graduate school. Whether he would graduate at the top of the class or not, the others around him assumed he was.

Cory knew not to argue with Ian. His word was usually the last and closed whatever subject was being debated.

Senior Ethics was probably, other than the lab work and curiously, Economics 101, the most interesting class Jimmy had taken in the last four years. Nuclear Physics was fascinating, but a known dead end as he had no intention of entering the nuclear power business. The trip to Fermi Lab and the radiation experiment they had done there had the kind of science fiction edge to make it cool enough to brag about, but nothing would sprout from it later.

But this lecture was nothing new to Jimmy. When he started cashing those two-thousand dollar checks he was headed straight to the department stores, to fill his closet with the clothes he could never afford before. No way was he wearing pocket protectors, navy blue blazers, oxfords, and white shirts. He had to wear things to show he had a personality and more importantly, money not only in his pocket, but in the bank. That was what all this study was leading to.

Three Pointers

Luxury boy
Stuck between sheets,
The funny numbers
On sheet upon sheet upon sheet,
Correct by instinct.

The life of no hardships
Has turned his speech
In circles, impenetrable;
The idle hours filled
With only his own thoughts.

Riddles, always the riddles,
The means to unravelling
This myriad fibered psyche,
Which when half solved
Never fails to prove
The exception to the rule;
That everyone has someone,
God gives all a second chance,
Love knows no boundaries;
This rule disproved again and again.

There are people who need lovers
To help provide their meat and shelter,
Others are needed.
The rest are playing
Musical human chairs,

Taking turns using and being used,
With always one left
Standing.

Luxury boy,
Standing in the knee-high weeds,
Spurting those apt to be
Usable, legitimate, digits,
Watching the chairs become sitters,
And the sitters, chairs,
Always adding more on, more on.

It would be many years before he wrote this poem. Theory had to become reality before it sprang forth from his subconscious. Until then he knew what he wanted to be, had a plan to get there, and had an idol to show him the way.

It was a fluke when he first saw Julius Erving on television in 1976. The Cubs game scheduled for this time slot had been rained out, and the network, in desperation, showed game 6 of the ABA finals, the Nets against the Nuggets, instead. His father had groaned and left Jimmy alone in the basement to watch the greatest game he would ever watch a professional athlete play, the only athlete worthy of his complete devotion. If he wasn't scoring on a high-flying dunk, he was snatching a rebound, passing to a teammate for an open shot, or erasing some hapless opponent's attempt to shoot a layup over him. He had heard of David Thompson, had seen him leap over seven-foot guys to block their most difficult hook shots, so when he saw this graceful creature with his even more graceful afro leap to swat away one of the incomparable leaper David Thompson's offerings, he knew what he was watching was beyond what he thought was physically possible.

The Nuggets, the favored squad filled with so many superstars they had played as a team in the All-Star game that year and won, were ahead by 22 points with 16 minutes left in the game, which in any other game Jimmy had watched meant it was over. But by this point he would watch Julius no matter what the score. That was when the Nets decided to employ an unheard of 1 -4 offense with Julius at the top of the key. Despite double teams, triple teams, the entire team swarming him, he took it to the hole time and time again, sometimes dishing, sometimes soaring all the way to the cup to score, and when the final buzzer sounded, the Nets had won by 6. Julius had 31 points, the lowest amount he scored in any game of the series, but had 19 rebounds, 5 assists, 5 steals, and 4 blocked shots, and Jimmy never wanted to play any other sport than basketball ever again, on any day or in any season.

This is not to say Jimmy had any intention of making any money playing basketball. The limits of his anatomy were too obviously visible for him to fool himself into that dream. But he could become as articulate, as self-assured, as well dressed and coifed, and as able to overcome the innumerable obstacles of life as Julius Erving. He could also be gracious in victory and defeat. He knew nothing could stand in his way if he kept his heart open and his soul full of the possibilities ahead of him. If Julius could do it, why couldn't he?

7. Three Lost Things

The result of the first game of the season was not as planned. Being the anointed favorites to win the All-University Championship was difficult enough, but playing a team named the Cunning Linguists made it nearly impossible to focus on playing defense, rebounding, or prudent shot selection. When all you think you need to do is show up, put five guys out there, and let it happen, it doesn't. You can't have a love affair by committee. You can't open it up to discussion, have running arguments between the bench and the starters, debate who should play the most minutes and who should be paired with whom during the game. Timeouts can't be shouting matches between teammates about the matchups, what offence to run against a zone, who is best suited to bring the ball up court when pressed, and whether the point guard is shooting too much or passing too hard.

All of that happened in the first half to the Goodfellas. The season before was chaotic, it in fact led to Tyrone and his now ex-roommate and ex-teammate needing to be separated after going toe to toe after a tough loss in the playoffs, to the addition of two white players, the aptly named Paul Carpenter and the less believably named Leroy Jones, and to Jimmy demanding to become the point guard, a position he had never played and was not best suited for but knew was necessary for the stability of the offense and the functionality of the defense. Those changes made for a better team, but the loss of their ridiculed coach, one of those too rotund to play and not quite knowledgeable enough to be taken too seriously, to a transfer at the end of the year was the most devastating blow of all. Especially since he was considered an afterthought at best and had been named coach only because he was a high school friend of Hal and Darrell, the team's founders.

The Linguists had played a tight zone out of necessity since they were short, slow, and couldn't put many points on the board. The only chance they had was to play like snails and work the ball around to their one scorer, a smooth and methodical jump shooter named Michael Davis, the kind of player who never spoke on the court except through his silky release, who could be stopped with a hand in his face but was deadly without one, and hope the game was low scoring enough to not get blown out. With an impatience the Cunning ones could have only dreamt of, and were not in the least expecting, the Goodfellas did everything perfectly right if they were trying to lose to a much less talented team. Not passing the ball to the open man, not setting up a high post or low post offense, not talking on defense or switching to make sure Michael Davis did not get open looks, and not blocking out under the basket, and in general not trusting each other enough to be able to wear their opponent down and instead blaming each other for every made shot by Michael and every missed opportunity by themselves.

When it was over, a horrible display to either watch or be part of, the score was a pitiful twenty-six to thirty, and the Cunning Linguists were wordless as they danced in circles congratulating themselves, yelling and whooping at their unexpected success. Even the name of the team told everyone they were not to be taken seriously, but here they were, having vanquished the mighty Goodfellas, everyone's pick as the most talented team on The Yard, and almost everyone's pick to somehow self-destruct, life imitating life.

Despite not having done enough to deserve being exhausted, Jimmy felt paralyzed from the effect of his incompetence as he sat in the top row of the bleachers, trying to accept this was not a bad dream and he was awake and hearing the snickers of the assembled throng in the gym, waiting for the next contest to begin. Michael Davis climbed the stairs and sat next to him, and Jimmy reached out his hand to congratulate him. They had played together the first two years of college and respected each other enough for Jimmy to not begrudge him for winning, and Michael to not gloat about what had just occurred.

"Good game, man," said Jimmy, with as much of a smile as he could muster.

"Naw, it wasn't," said Michael, shaking his head honestly. "Those guys," he said pointing to his teammates, "are a bunch of clowns. You should have wiped the floor with us. You guys need a coach."

Michael loved the sport enough to enjoy basketball played at its best, and he did not enjoy playing against the ineptitude that had allowed him to be the victor. True love does not appreciate being mocked. Jimmy had no answer. He looked down at his shoes, lost in his own dejection. Michael sat for a while longer, then pulled on his sweats before patting Jimmy on the back as he rose.

"Catch you later, Jimmy," he said as he trotted down to the floor level.

"Yeah, see ya," responded Jimmy.

Once they had seen this scene ending, Hal and Tyrone stepped up to crowd their teammate.

"Was he rubbing it in?" asked Tyrone, his soul still filled with anger even more than embarrassment. He was wondering why Jimmy had sat there and taken what he assumed had just happened. Hal was thinking the same thing but let his more extroverted friend voice it.

"Not really," said Jimmy. "He was giving me good advice. We need a coach."

Hal looked at Jimmy and wanted to argue. Michael had been rubbing it in whether Jimmy realized it or not. But then stopped himself, as he couldn't deny the wisdom.

"You mean we really did need that fat fucker?" asked Tyrone, who had never been very pleased with Hal and Darrell's selection of their leader.

Jimmy stared hard at Tyrone. It was Jimmy who nicknamed him "Large Louis," after all, and had not taken him any more seriously than necessary. It was Jimmy who ignored his suggestions during timeouts and told the other players what to do as they walked on the court. He let the intensity in his eyes answer Tyrone's question.

Three Pointers

I.

Ali Baba had forty thieves,
Mohammed had his mountain.
All he had was the shirt on his back
And a hope and a promise, and a dream.

The light shone on him as he rose,
Fair indeed to all those who gazed.
Those who denied were the most entranced,
They bargained in the shadows for a glimpse.

It was subtle how those looks changed him,
The three things he brought with him were hidden away.
The shirt replaced by more extravagant means,
So that he could change the looks.

II.

One day he woke up upset in his soul,
He searched 'til he found the right thought.
Could it be in the quest of the eye
He had forgotten where he stashed what he brought?

His soul stared at the ground in disgust,
"I've come this far and forgotten why I came,
And it makes me wonder if I ever knew.
I must have a new goal to go on."

So he stopped all external and folded inside,
Turned his imagination loose on his mind.
Found his greatest desire for fate to bestow
Was to bring the three lost back to his heart.

"What about Grassman?" wondered Hal aloud, pointing to a short, always chattering white kid with straggly hair and an even stragglier moustache.

Tyrone's response was to roar in laughter. Grassman was a gym rat who hardly ever played himself. He showed up to all the intramural games or whenever he knew the best players would be in the gym. On the rare occasions when not enough guys were there to make up two teams, he would descend from his perch in the bleachers to join in, and his game was barely up to the level where he could be trusted to be passed the ball, and he was automatically assigned to guard the weakest guy on the opponent's squad. If someone made the mistake of letting him stick a guy with any talent or size what-so-ever, he would quickly correct their mistake and find his low water mark to defend, but normally he would wait until the best guys were worn out and left the gym to play, when the lead footed and uncoordinated took over. However, since he was always there and quick to compliment the more talented around him, he was a friend to all the ballers on The Yard.

"You know he'll show up to all the games," said Hal to further convince the skeptical Tyrone.

Tyrone could not argue with that, so he shrugged his shoulders to affirm his agreement.

"I'll go talk to him," said Hal with finality. The decision had been made.

Grassman had been there on the day the bodybuilders had taken over the court. It was in the early evening on a day in the first semester, when it was still warm and light enough outside for the best ballers to be out and about strolling the campus courting females instead of basketballs, so he was able to be picked on a side. They were playing four on four, scrubs against scrubs, when four massive hulks lumbered onto the court from the weight room and called next. There was a bodybuilders' competition in town that week, and these were some of the professionals, with muscles bulging from places normal people don't have them, and where normal people did, they were too humungous to be believed. As they were playing half court, Make-It-Take-It, and fouls had to be argued and were not accepted without aggression, the bodybuilders won their first game by crowding around the basket, muscling their smaller opponents away from the lane, and dominating rebound after rebound, despite their lack of touch and inability to leave the Earth with both feet at the same time.

Jimmy strolled into the gym and watched the action as he stretched and ran in place to warm up, waiting for the better talented competition he knew would arrive once the sun fell behind the shadows of night. The big boys were rough, mouthy and so filled with testosterone as they manhandled their weaker opponents it morphed into a challenge to Jimmy he could not let pass, like a man in a bar who must fight for a woman's honor. He could no longer quell his passion when one of the big men said as they scored the seventh and last point, "Us body builders are the best athletes in the world! We can hold this court all night if we want to. No way you puny girls can beat us!"

With that Jimmy rose from his stretch and said to Grassman, the only guy he knew from the bunch of newly defeated players hanging their heads at the taunts of the

Goliaths standing around the basket laughing, "Let me run with you this time."

One of the others gladly gave up his spot, and the game was on. Games of Make-It-Take-It are games of domination. The winners of the last game take the ball at the key, and if they make their first basket they get the ball again, and again, and the opponents must stop them if they are ever to obtain possession. There are no three-second calls allowed, so the basket can be constantly crowded by the offense, and the only way to get them out of there is to push them out. Since each of the massive men was at least two hundred fifty pounds of steroid fueled muscle, shirtless to show each mound of meat scrupulously sculpted to their frames through hours of lifting weights heavier than two of their opponents together, they stood under the basket like trees along a river bank, rooted to their spots without the possibility of being moved.

Jimmy knew what had to be done, and that was to fly above the treetops, taking his chances against the forearms reaching to swat him like a fly in the kitchen during the heat of August. The big boys scored the first four, but when one of their harsh attempts at a shot clanged against the backboard and recoiled far enough away to be gathered by a mere mortal, Jimmy sprang into action. A corner jump shot came first, then another, which forced one of the trees to spread out to that spot, leaving a gap for a drive for a midrange shot at the elbow. Then a pass to a surprised Grassman led to a set shot at the key which smacked hard against the backboard before falling in to tie the score. A few misses by each and one make led to a five to five score, and when Jimmy reached an offensive rebound, gliding high above the muscle men, he took a hard step to the basket before they could react and laid it in, making the score six-five and a point away from victory.

The head honcho of the mountains, trying to coerce another victory by challenging him to a fatal mistake, called out, "You better not try that again, Stick Man! Under the basket is my territory! Come in here again and you'll pay for it."

Jimmy smiled as he stood with the ball at the top of the key. Times like this are to be treasured, as they are the only ones in which true love can be expressed without any doubts to its veracity. He faked right, dribbled with his left, and jumped directly at the taunting hulk, soaring through the air on a collision course with the massive obstacle he knew would neither yield nor give quarter. The ball rolled off his fingertips like a melody off the tongue of a troubadour, so lightly and in tune with the universe it was sure to find its home in the heavens, calm in the knowing what came next was of no consequence. The wallop that came was powerful and well timed and succeeded in its goal to blow the dust speck floating toward it far out of bounds and tumbling against the wall next to the water fountain, feet up, face down, and elbows out wide attempting to absorb the contact.

"That's game!!" shouted Grassman, the only evidence Jimmy had of the outcome of his boldness from his position facing the water spout. "Damn Jimmy," said his friend as he rushed over to see what had been broken, and after finding nothing had been, yelled out; "You'll take anyone to the hole!!"

8. Excerpt from the Unpublished Memoirs of Houdini

The atomic world may appear to be an infinitesimally small version of the planetary systems and galaxies we can see for ourselves on a clear night, but it is quite shocking to find, when forced to study it, the atomic world induces the exact opposite of the calm and peace stargazing does. That's because the atomic world doesn't care about gravity. It runs on electrical forces on its surface, from a calm distance, with its negative electrons spinning around its positive protons. But when your professor asks you to consider the forces that bind the positive particles of the nucleus, it leads to quantum mechanical equations and prior theories becoming obsolete, atomic weights changing as light is emitted, and the conclusion protons are made up of parts themselves, and there are other forces, weak and strong nuclear ones, entangled in the consequences of relativity.

The course was called Nuclear Physics 505 and the five at the beginning meant it was a graduate level class and Jimmy was not required to take it, but he did anyway because he'd always wanted to and now in his last semester he had the time. It was labelled Nuclear because it was the study of the nucleus of atoms, the core of everything, the building blocks of the universe's unimaginable trillions upon trillions upon trillions upon trillions of kilograms of mass. It was labelled Physics because it was the study of the properties of matter and energy of the nucleus, not its chemistry or biology. Deciphering the math was like being a small child laughing and running through a garden maze and then needing to find your way out wailing in terror and dizziness as the vines close in and the rain pours down. Bursting into the sunlight to find the grace infused within, leading to sub atomic particles and multitudes of new forces and interactions, quarks and gluons and the combinations yielding neutrons and protons, the strange art of creation.

So today was the lecture on radioactivity, what it physically is and how it happens. The three types: Alpha, when helium escapes; Beta, with its positrons and neutrinos; and Gamma's high energy photon, all fused together or ripped apart to a symphony of elegant equations; their quirky decay paths and unique half-lives leading to ever more theories and mathematical suppositions well beyond the standard calculations of mass, energy, and levels of threat to human life. The professor, speaking with the air of a wizard conjuring spells, said, "Nuclear decay is more truly described as nuclear disintegration, as this much more closely matches the math involved…"

Jimmy put his hand up. That's all, just put his hand up. There was a guy standing in front of him, a big solid guy, no doubt, but nothing special was going on. The two of them were standing at the free throw line, waiting for the ball to be brought up court, and the big man took a half step back, into the space Jimmy was occupying, so he put his hand up.

It was a warm spring day and the doors to the gym were open to the breezes and the fresh scents wafting in from the parking lot. Jimmy was playing with his company team, like he had for the last five years, and was now in his early thirties with a wife and two children and a mortgage, so this once a week game was the only time he was inside a gym. There was no time for shooting free throws or running around a track or exercise regimens. This was his only fitness related activity of the week, and as such he greedily anticipated it during the off seasons, and lived for it during the season. Of course there were rec leagues like this one throughout the year, but he and his work crew agreed they would not participate in more than two per year and take six months off to recuperate, as most of them had hectic schedules and weren't getting in any more gym time than Jimmy.

The teams they battled were trending younger and younger, less skilled but more athletic, and it had been a few years since they had won their one and only city championship, but the FunRun team was still hanging in there. The summer league was played in a community gym in Tierrasanta, and children on jungle gyms screaming in delight could be heard on the playground outside through the open gym doors. Maybe that is why Jimmy didn't hear the crack in his hand when the big man stepped into him and he put his hand against his opponent's back. He felt it bend at a weird angle, but then the pass came, and he had to defend. There were only a couple of minutes left in the half, and they were down two points and fighting to keep the score close.

The second half remained tight, they had maintained their resolve on the defensive end as was their mantra, but in the waning minutes the fatigue caught up to them, no shots were launched with enough energy to penetrate the rim, and the younger bodies against them were able to make a couple of shots late after offensive rebounds. As they were doing more often these days than in days past, they cheered themselves on their dedication to making the effort, praised the way their bodies felt after the exertion, expressed their near certainty that next week the outcome would be positive, and shook hands and limped to their cars knowing, even if they made love to her as often as they had so seemingly long ago, the girl they loved would never love them back again. She might tease them, pity them with unexpected affection on those lucky days when every shot seemed to fall, but even those would be rare occasions and the typical day would end sore, aching and embarrassed at best; and racked with pain, braced by crutches, or rushed to a local urgent care hospital at less than best.

Jimmy wasn't thinking of driving directly to urgent care as he waved goodbye to his teammates and walked to his car. There was not a pain in his body. He felt only the emptiness, not so much at the defeat but at the complete expulsion of energy from his body. This game had emptied him. He did not feel fuller from the experience than he felt drained by its effect on his internal organs. He opened the door, stuck the key in the ignition, and clutched the steering wheel with both hands to take a deep breath. Instead of breathing deep, Jimmy let out a cry as his right hand folded around the wheel in a way it wasn't designed to, and the pain it caused was searing. Jimmy quickly spread his fingers and held up his hand to make sure he didn't touch anything with it by accident.

Then he drove home. The house was full of people, and food was being eaten, and children called for attention, and a shower needed to be taken. After a meal struggled through one-handed Jimmy finally had a chance to sit on the couch next to his father-in-law, who said to him matter-of-factly, "You know you broke your hand, don't you Jimmy?"

"Broke it?" Jimmy responded quite incredulously. "I'm mean it hurts, but I can handle it. If it was broken wouldn't I be in agony?"

"I'm not a pain expert, Jimmy, but I know a broken hand when I see one."

His father-in-law saw no need to discuss it further and turned his attention to the television, leaving Jimmy to ponder whether the throbbing in his hand would go away or increase. It couldn't be broken. In all these many years of playing basketball Jimmy had never broken a bone, had never walked with crutches, had never needed surgery because of playing the sport he loved. It had always nurtured him, uplifted him, strengthened his body and his spirit. He had fallen face first, been thrown down at awkward angles on shoulders and shins, piled on until nearly crushed, elbowed in the head, the neck, the torso, kneed in places indelicate and delicate, knocked out of the air by swinging and locked forearms, twisted ankles, dislocated fingers, had his toes smashed and his arches exposed as frauds, but he had never broken anything. He couldn't believe it, even though his hand was ballooning so quickly he could watch it swelling with the naked eye.

It was confirmed the next morning at the clinic, but Jimmy himself was convinced as soon as he woke up and his hand was more swollen and sore than any limb had ever been his life. He drove past the closest places to the one he knew was used to make the casts, where the real experts worked. The X-Ray technician shook his head when he saw the pictures.

"You broke it in three places," said the chuckling man. "And you waited until the next day to come in? It didn't hurt or something?"

"Not that bad," said Jimmy. Not as bad as the shock of breaking it standing still, not the result of a violent collision, or even a stumble.

"You fell on it?" asked the guy, just to make Jimmy feel worse.

"No, I was just standing there. It must be time for me to start playing softball."

"I'm X-Raying softball players just about every day. Basketball's worse, but a lot more people play softball."

"That's reassuring," said Jimmy. "Will the cast just be on my hand? How long?"

The man laughed. "From just below the elbow. I'm not the doctor, but probably 6 to 8 weeks."

"Why so long!!??" asked Jimmy, knowing he was in for long journey of answering 'how'd you do it' questions, and laughter at his misfortune, and was saddened the affair was ending so badly. After last years' hernia, coming with a plop as Jimmy ran down the court unimpeded in a league game ten months before, he had not been deterred. The doctor told him playing basketball had not really caused it, only hastened it, and that was probably a good thing, as it would heal more soundly since he was younger. But if that was a warning, this was the door-slamming-in-his-face type of rebuke he was not able to deny. It was time to accept it. She had left him for others, many others. He had heard the snickers reserved for the cuckold on the court for years now.

To make things clear:
The only things I have never been able to accomplish
Are the ones I never believed I could do to start with.
Mind over matter is a matter of the mind.
You shackled me by pointing out how my shortcomings caused
you to suffer,
To speak of principles was futile.
I could dive off a bridge others used as a suicide jump,
But drown in a sea of regret if you felt slighted.
I knew I could escape from any manmade trap,
You bound me without a single knot.
This artist could not have been more guiled by the blow off.
I did not believe it was a magician's trick,
So I remain ensnared.
It matters little the death I cannot escape
Can be dealt by a blow received in any simple barroom brawl
By men too drunk to believe they can be hurt.
Trust me, I won't ever let go.

"Don't get mad at me," said the technician. "You're the one still playing basketball at your age."

"...Today we are going to study the path of nuclear disintegration of Cobalt 60. Its starts with a nucleus of 60/27 and undergoes a beta process which results in Nickel 60/28* excited, that then further decays through two separate photon emissions to achieve stable Nickel 60/28. You can copy the path from what I've drawn on the blackboard. It shows the half-life and the resulting energy releases, so you'll need it. Use the formulas in Chapter 7 to calculate mass, energy emitted, and current radioactivity level after 2 years of 10 grams of Cobalt 60..."

9. Anniversary

If you've never been in love before, you don't know what the feeling is that is immersing your soul until a long time after you've fallen in it. It was not for years, long after the affair had begun to fade, that Jimmy realized what had happened, when he had become enraptured, and it was like finding a lost toy after he'd stopped looking. But in the fifth grade it was just something to do after school for a couple of weeks, along with half of the other boys in his class, and it took place on the carpeted floor of the gym class, with only enough room around the court to fit in the water fountain and ball rack.

As he looked back on it, that was the first day of his life he had control of his health. He had always been an active boy, but was often racked with illnesses which had resulted in more than one hospital stay, and he had felt the steel edge of the surgeon's knife before ever holding a pencil in his hand as a schoolboy. Sports were no mystery to him, having three years of little league baseball in his rear view, but basketball was something he had only played in his gravel driveway with his older brother and the boys on his block, as there were no organized leagues for players so young. The idea of playing a sport indoors was intriguing, as his main complaint about baseball was the cold, rain, and biting wind of the spring which could last until the Fourth of July, but as he ran around with his classmates doing the drills and listening to the teachers bark out commands, he began to see the difference between this new endeavor and his former as one in which his creativity and independent thinking could be brought to the fore. There was more than one right way to do things, and you had to think on your feet to decide which to do. Bounce pass? Chest pass? Dribble one step and then pass? All could be correct, and all could be wrong. And everyone could do everything. It wasn't up to one guy to pitch, and the others to stand around and wait. There wasn't one guy batting while everyone else sat and watched.

But the magic elixir, the love potion that changed his frail, sickly body into the still rail thin, but rail strong bundle of vitality it became, was the wind sprints the teacher doled out at the end of the first practice and in increasing volume as the days passed. Jimmy's illnesses, the weakness of his immune system, the need for supplements and extreme caution when eating anything too complex, all came from his metabolism being too sedentary. His guts needed to be moved, jostled, strained to the point of exhaustion as they were during that first round of wind sprints to speed them up and evacuate all the toxins which had been loitering in his body for all the years before, and after that practice Jimmy had the best time in a toilet he had in his life, and the subsequent regularity he gained, slowly at first, by his teen years had eradicated any hint of disease. And that was that. Never again did Jimmy play organized baseball.

We never made love,
We just shared what we had,
And that's alright with me.

Set out to make a future
As it unfolds naturally
We shared a destiny.

I can smile at you inside
When I cannot raise my eyes
In a world passing by dispassionately,

And it tickles me to tell you.

The Q's had a Valentine's Day tournament, and of course the Goodfellas were invited. After losing the game to the Cunning Linguists they had brought Grassman on as coach and hadn't had a close game since. They were expected to run the table and win the All-U's and winning this tourney would be a bauble to pick up along the way, but the Q's were not about to lose their own tournament. They imported a group of studs from anywhere they could find them. They just had to be a Q, be related to a Q, or be over six foot six and have been seen playing basketball at some point in their life by a Q. When the Strollers, the most popular team among the campus ladies, found out about the Q's imports, they added some guys too, one being Keith Kelly, the freshman star of the varsity baseball team who would someday become a real All Star centerfielder in the big leagues, and another guy whose older shorter brother was on the team, and his older brother was six four.

That was who the Goodfellas ran into in the semi-finals. The Q's had not only stacked their team, they had stacked the brackets as well, making themselves the top seed and giving themselves no competition until the final game, and putting all the contenders in the other bracket to fight it out. The Strollers and Goodfellas had not had much trouble getting through their first opponents, with Keith amazing everyone with the superior athletic skills he possessed - despite his inferior height he was unstoppable. The Goodfellas did not import anyone, they played their normal guys.

The game got chippy very early. There were too many egos, too much unbridled testosterone, and more importantly, too many cute girls watching a few feet away. It seemed all the ones Jimmy had fantasized about were there. All his muses. All the other guys' as well.

It hadn't taken very long for the Goodfellas to realize no one on their team could stay in front of Keith. Within the first five minutes it was clear when Jimmy, Paul Carpenter, the white freshman with such a pure shooting stroke he had almost made the varsity team, and Mike Marsh, the team's best one on one defender, were all left dizzy watching Mr. Kelly squirt past them untouched on his way to the basket. The only one with a chance was Jerry Davis, who was just as short and thick as Keith but maybe three quarters as quick and strong on a good day, the backup point guard. In a time out after falling behind by 6 points, all slashes by Keith to the hole, a new strategy was worked out. Jerry would guard Keith, and not try to stay in front of him, but instead to channel him to one side of the court or the other. It would then be the task of the other defenders to pick him up mid-slash, because it was also recognized by those in the Goodfella's huddle Keith would never pass the ball after making his move, he'd always put up a shot. And great athlete or not, a guy five foot eight going to the hole against taller guys who could jump and were waiting on him was not anything other than an act of extreme, towering ego. Jimmy could relate to that, but he knew his limitations and would pass once he knew his shot was going to be blocked, but Keith refused to admit this and never thought it could happen. That was the way to stop him, to use his own ego against him.

And so it went for the rest of the first half. Keith would go strong to the hole and at least half of them would get thrown. In his mind they were mostly fouls, but the refs were not in his mind. He reached his breaking point when after a very sweet crossover left Jerry behind and screaming to Jimmy for help that wasn't coming in his eyes, then past a befuddled Darrell Everett on the base line, and on to a majestic finger roll as he twisted his body gracefully in mid-air, where Jimmy had been calculating he would arrive and was springing into the air. The ball rolled off Keith's fingers and into Jimmy's hand. Instead of catching it as he should have and starting the fast break, his adrenaline took control and swatted the ball far out of bounds, behind the basket, to the thunderous cheers and laughter of the crowd, almost drowning out Keith's response.

"That was a fucking foul!!" he growled out in anger.

When Jimmy turned his back and started collecting the high fives he had coming to him, Keith reacted by grabbing the ball and throwing it half strength at the back of Jimmy's head. Not hard enough to hurt him but plenty hard enough to start the fight he wanted to start. Jimmy reacted with a smile, the kind killers use before pulling their gun, and rolled the ball back slowly to Keith. That was not what Keith expected. Jimmy was supposed to have charged at him with his fists balled. So he threw it again, this time full strength, but since Jimmy was looking this time he merely caught it and rolled it back again. Tyrone, who knew there should be a fight happening by this point, decided he would do what Keith wanted, but by the time he started his move the refs stepped in and called a halt to the impending brawl.

The second half was no less tense, even though the Strollers stretched their lead to ten by the time it was over. Every loose ball was challenged and diving on the floor was a common occurrence but in the end the size and depth of the Strollers won out. The game was sealed, unbeknownst to them at the time, when Keith Kelly was injured early in the second half, allowing the Strollers to focus on the fact they had three players taller than any of the Goodfellas and should be going inside and letting them dominate. He was injured when he dove for a ball that was tipped away from another and smashed his left eye into Jimmy's shoulder, perfectly placed there in anticipation of Keith's face's arrival, as the ball bounded toward him and he could see Keith's upcoming trajectory. All he had to do was bend over, pick up the ball, and wait.

10. Indoor Thoughts

Indoor thoughts,
From an outdoor mind;
Up front honesty,
Whispered from behind;
Such sweet favors,
Given though unkind;
Once upon a thought upon a smile.

More than just a guest,
Less than the most you could possibly want to be.
Somewhere in the rest,
Is someone you know could fall short further.
Never be distressed,
('Inside is where I try to find', digested thought of a constipated mind)
One thing I detest,
Don't give me that sour look, please smile.

Fifty-yard dash,
Through an alley, underneath a façade.
Could be smooth,
Flustered heart cold as a cod.
Be not humble,
Go into the fire with a rod.
As you exit,
For the sake of God, please smile.

That one did it. It wasn't his best, his most heartfelt, his most meaningful, was not dedicated to the muse he most desired, but it rhymed, sort of. Not many of the others did, no matter what his intentions when starting them. For that reason this one couldn't be hidden. It had to be read by at least one other person. It couldn't go unnoticed into the folder stacked discreetly amongst the piles of other folders filled with scribbles and sketches, notes from classes digested and excreted semesters before. Eyes other than his had to dance across the paper to catch the song in the syllables.

So that would be his gift. A strange and wonderful gift. A Pandora's box of delights for the eyes of his muses, silently and stealthily distributed after nightfall to their doors and mailboxes, always to be discovered after he had slipped into the same shadows the words he spat onto the pages were spawned in the first place, like smoke drifting into the nostrils of his creativity from a mystical vent. They would be amused. Of that he could be sure. Maybe they would be titillated. Maybe they would be entranced and search for him. It wouldn't matter if they did, since by not being a suspect he could never be unmasked. If the pattern that had been established long ago prevailed, others would benefit by confessing to their accusers that yes, they had put their pen to the paper being waved in front of them and written the words their tortured hearts demanded be poured out to their beloved. Someone, at least, would get laid.

Since Bradley did not have a football team, the student body craved the start of basketball season with an intensity schools focused on the gridiron in the fall could never achieve. The pent-up energy had to have some sort of competitive release, and by 1980 it had reached the point intramural basketball season, which was usually restricted to the spring semester only, was given a head start by the holding of an open to all comer's basketball tournament in November. And since there were no football games to provide on-campus social events during the fall to see and be seen at, and the campus was surrounded by even less excitement, as it was surrounded by the city of Peoria, the games were played in front of increasing numbers of students as the brackets narrowed to the finals.

Their run through the tourney was impressive enough, in fact was not a surprise to those who made their second home, if not their first, in Haussler Hall, but the game which established the Goodfellas as the favorite to win it all in the spring was the semifinal against the TKE's. The TKE's were the defending All-U champions, having beaten the former champions, the Campus Kings, who had ridden the back of the legendary scholar-baller Shack to the title for the three years prior, in the biggest upset in the history of Bradley intramurals. It might have not been expected by those who watched and wasn't the way Shack envisioned his final pre-graduation game ending, but that game hadn't been close, as the TKE's cruised. They had the biggest frontline Bradley intramurals had ever seen, and guards who could shoot. And since the Holiday Tournament was their first action since their triumph last spring, the TKE's hadn't lost a game since, and a big crowd came out to watch them ace their last test before the highly anticipated rematch against the reformed, recharged and Shack-less Campus Kings in the final.

By this game Jimmy was growing into his role as point guard. Everyone already knew he was unstoppable as an off-guard, but the point is a different skill set, and more importantly a different mindset. An off-guard must have a "shoot first" ego, and a point guard must have a "score first" mentality. Both must be driven by the desire to win, but one prefers to play solo while the other must lead an orchestra. A good point guard must always think about defense and floor balance and a good off-guard must always be putting himself in a position to use his athletic skills to best effect. To be able to switch from one philosophy to another is not something most players can do well, and that question must always be answered when the transition is attempted. Can a guy able to score at will overcome his ego and pass to someone not as skilled to be in a better position to defend when the shot is missed, or made, for that matter? Can a guy pass up a shot he knows he can make to give a big man who he needs to stay motivated to block out and rebound a chance to score? Does he know when to take over and be selfish with the ball when that is what his team needs? This game answered all those questions about Jimmy absolutely.

The TKE's beating the Campus Kings the year before had caused the almost mandatory segregation of the best intramural teams on the campus to end. The intramural league itself was segregated with the all-white fraternities having their own division and the remainder of the campus in the other division. It was not segregation based on race directly, more on class, but with the fraternities themselves being segregated, and no black fraternities having the money to join the Greek Council, the Frat Division was all white by default. Every year for the past ten, at least, a team from the Open Division, usually 100% black, won the All-U tournament, which pitted the top two Open Division teams against the top two frat teams in a four-team bracket. But when the frat boys won with the huge front line the Campus Kings could not match, it initiated a recruiting war among the Open Division elite teams for the top white players not already bound by a trio of Greek letters.

The Goodfellas may have done better than anyone at integrating. When Jimmy joined the team the year before, there was no way a white player would even be considered, and when Hal and Tyrone approached him with the idea of adding Leroy Jones, a player Jimmy had played against a couple of times in pickup games, he was not pleased.

"Man, you know this guy can play," said Hal after hearing Jimmy's totally negative reaction.

Jimmy didn't have a good answer for that one. He had been the only black player on a team of whites in high school, and the idea of playing on an all-black team for the first and only time in his life, and the unfiltered camaraderie he felt for the first time on a team was hard for him to conceive giving up.

"Well," said Jimmy, conflicted with the thoughts coursing through him, "I don't like him." Then he had to admit, as his thought process reached its conclusion, "Mainly because he's cocky. I can't stop him though."

The idea of a white guy named Leroy Jones was bad enough, but he didn't look like a baller either. He was slightly taller than Jimmy, and thicker in a way that didn't look athletic no matter how long you stared at it and from what angle, but within that thickness was a core strength which kept taller, bigger guys off him and allowed him to get off shots under the basket instead of it resulting in a white forehead with "Wilson" stamped on it.

That had been Jimmy's thought. Even though Leroy was slightly bigger he could not jump that high and was at least a half step slower, so there was no way this guy should be able to score against him, especially at will if he got position down low, but that is what had happened. Instead of letting him get the ball and swatting it away as he first thought, his only defense turned out to be denying the guy the ball in the first place, and hoping he didn't get the rebound, because Leroy knew how to block out. It turned out Leroy played in the Chicago public league as a 6-foot 2-inch center, which means he was used to playing against guys a lot bigger, stronger, and able to leap much higher than Jimmy could ever do, and he was not to be intimidated by anyone in the Bradley University intramural program. Even still, he couldn't crack the Goodfellas starting five.

Paul Carpenter was another matter. Jimmy had seen him in the gym before, not playing pickup, just shooting gem after gem of brilliant jump shots, all jewels perfectly cut by arc and rotation. Jimmy had to ask when the kid wouldn't join in a pickup game and found out Paul was a freshman walk-on trying out for the varsity, a few days removed from a town of less than three hundred, with more corn and cows surrounding him than people, and his only past time being shooting jumper after jumper. As it turned out he made it past the first cuts but did not make the final one, in fact may have been the last man left not standing. That left him without a team to play for in November, and with Jimmy switching to point guard, put the Goodfellas in the position of needing a shooting guard to start alongside him. After the first couple of games coming off the bench and proving he may be the best pure shooter on the campus not in a varsity uniform, he made his first start against the TKE's.

The game was tight, from beginning to end. Neither team could stretch the lead to more than six points. This was the type of game the Goodfellas played most of the time. When they were shooting well, which was rare, they blew teams out. When they weren't, which was normal, games were close because no team could score much against them. Scores would be 60 to 40 if they were hot, and 44 to 40 if they weren't. This game was one of the 40 pointers. The TKE's zone was impressive, and the amount of effort taken to penetrate it limited the energy of those working against it to finish with the ball falling through the rim. The Goodfellas played man to man exclusively, and with Jimmy and Hal constantly shouting out the coming picks and screens, the TKE's were locked down even worse. Therefore scores of shots were missed, and rebounding was the key to the game, and Tyrone, Hal, and Darrell had just enough of a quickness advantage without giving up too much size to balance out the bigger TKE's, boiling the key to winning or losing the game down to guard play.

As the game wore on it was established the Goodfellas had the edge amongst the little guys. The zone couldn't hide the TKE's lack of quickness, and more importantly, lack of creativity to break down the Goodfellas' web of defenders, and Jimmy directed the Goodfellas' offense by cutting partially through the zone forcing to react, then passing the ball to the open man for the shot. It was easy after he had danced his way to the hoop in the first half, taking all five of his opponents to the basket. Jimmy used that psychologically damaging event to play the TKE zone like a jazz quintet. He never again drove into the lane with the intent of scoring himself, but the TKE's were totally committed to never letting it happen again and over-committed people to stop what wasn't coming. That meant whenever Jimmy penetrated the zone someone was open. After giving Tyrone and Daryl their chances, he found Paul Carpenter on the left baseline, open for a jumper, and he could tell as the ball rotated perfectly through the air to splash through the net without bothering the rim Paul was not going to miss any baseline jumpers that day. Jimmy had been in that zone before and knew exactly what it looked like.

First it was a simple move straight between the top defenders, angling to his left like a lefthander is supposed to do, he waited until the left base line guy decided whether to take a step forward, uncovering Paul in the corner, or take the chance of Jimmy driving all the way to the basket. He stepped forward, Jimmy flipped the pass to Paul, and Paul fired off a shot any sniper would be proud of.

The next time Jimmy split the two men on the right side, high and low. Hal made a sharp cut down the lane, bringing the base line man up to cut the angle of that pass off, but leaving a more difficult, and therefore more rewarding, bounce pass down the base line to Paul available.

Jimmy took a forearm to the forehead for doubting this one was going in and circling under the basket for a rebound that wasn't necessary, courtesy of one of the TKE big men, who smiled afterwards in the way big guys do to let little guys know there is more coming if they come under the basket again.

The third one resulted in him being chastised by his own teammate. Striding down the lane again, Jimmy had a choice to pass straight ahead to Tyrone, who had his man pinned under the basket, or make a leaping, twisting pass to Paul in his magic spot, after having curled around the defenders on his way through the air. He chose the latter, and Paul rewarded him by releasing another object into an orbit as sure in its trajectory as Halley's Comet that did not worry anyone about its ultimate destination by clanking against the far side of the rim as it passed through.

"I was open underneath, man!!" shouted Tyrone as he watched the ball floating through the air.

After watching the ball go where he knew it would go, Jimmy trotted up the court with his angry teammate and replied, "Until he misses, I'm feeding him the ball."

Now that he had seen the ball splashing through, Tyrone could not argue.

And with that established, plus a few slashes by Hal Jimmy rewarded by putting the ball on his fingertips at his point of rising for the goal, and some timely offensive rebounding and control of the defensive glass, the Goodfellas were up by four with two minutes left. This was a position they had failed in enough times when the TKE's fouled Jimmy after he clutched a defensive rebound to stop the clock and put him on the free throw line, the murmurs started in the crowd, loud enough for Jimmy to hear as he walked down the court. "They're gonna choke," was the opinion of the majority, and a near consensus among the frat brothers.

Jimmy knew all the things he had done to this point in the game would turn to dust and consoling pats on the back after another hard-fought defeat if he didn't show extreme leadership at this exact second. He turned to his teammates and saw the anxious looks in their eyes, like they were also staring into the near future and seeing a collapse, same as the crowd. Any trace of fear in Jimmy left and was replaced by anger, and that anger was coated in a cocky proclamation.

"All we gotta do is make our free throws, and we've got this game won!!"

"Yeah," responded a frat boy in the stands. "And that is why you Goodfellas are about to lose!!" He had the ultimate confidence of past experiences coming out of his mouth as the words flowed. Everyone could hear it, especially Jimmy as he walked slowly down the court, since he was the one to whom the words were directed. Everyone knew what word he would have liked to substitute for "Goodfellas," and Jimmy was just the specific one about to choke.

Jimmy responded with a broad smile, and there was one positive response from the crowd. This game was so important Sonny Mathis had driven over that morning to watch it. He turned to Pat Hampton, sitting amongst a group of his fellow TKE's, not playing, as he was not allowed because he was the star pitcher on the varsity baseball team, and said, "He's gonna make 'em both, ain't he, Egg?"

He had hoped it would rile his former high school classmate to have his old high school nickname revealed to his college group, but he didn't react that way. Maybe it would have as a freshman, but as a senior he was at ease in any campus situation. In what was a complete surprise to his frat brothers, he responded, "Of course he will."

The first one dropped through the net with a slight touch of the rim before if fell through, and Jimmy made an exaggerated face to show everyone how displeased he was it had touched anything except the cords, like the shot falling was never in question and he was more concerned with the style. He could tell by the lift in the other Goodfellas' shoulders he had accomplished with that face what he intended, he expected to make his free throws, and so should they. It was about confidence, and Jimmy had enough to share with them if they took it.

The guy in the stands who had predicted failure before changed his mind and shouted, "Looks like you fouled the wrong one!!"

The second fell without touching iron. The confidence gained by making those free throws translated to the defensive end, and the TKE's were not allowed a credible shot again. They were reduced to fouling after their misses, and the only scoring from that point on were free throws, one by Tyrone and two by Darrell, until the horn sounded.

11. A Mile of Fantasy

Stolen kisses. The most enjoyable thing of all about playing basketball, to Jimmy anyway, was not scoring baskets, even though that was quite enjoyable, no doubt, and was the ultimate purpose of the game. It was not winning games or dominating opponents, which was a good thing as most of the teams he played on weren't prolific at either, and it wasn't even the friends and teammates he spent countless hours on countless courts sweating with. It wasn't showing off to the girls. More than any of these thrills - and let there be no doubt every one of the things described above was exalting - it was thievery that brought on the most intense climaxes. Stealthy clutches of things not his nor intended to be his, and best of all the broad daylight thuggery of the blocked shot. The horror in the eye of the helpless victim made even sweeter by the taller the man he was leaping over, the more beautiful the move he was obliterating, and the more onlookers there to bear witness to the hole shot through the ego of the opponent.

And therefore it could be dangerous. Men and sports intersect at the ego. The hormones of aggression were essential to our ascendance as a species and this ancient compulsion is best expressed in modern times in the competition provided by sports, but at its core is ultimately expressed in brutal violence. Our sports are translated in our minds into mild forms of warfare that conveniently only occasionally result in the deaths of the warriors but allow us to rejoice in their victories with the same tumult as when the soldiers come marching down the wide avenues with masses of confetti drifting down from the windows above. But the ego must be protected at all costs when defeated. Defeats in sports can be translated by bruised egos into defeats in life, and to avoid that outcome an escalation in violence is demanded. Narrow escapes notwithstanding.

Jerry Davis was a good-hearted soul, always eager to smile and to please. He had the undisciplined love of life and the lack of direction most youths from fatherless, disadvantaged backgrounds have, and those without a father are always disadvantaged, no matter their income bracket, but he had hope in abundance. If he had only been a foot taller or a step and a half quicker, he could have become one of the many Chicago ghetto athlete success stories that blossom in neighborhoods like this once a decade, but he had to settle for a shot at an education and a good enough rep to allow him access to a spot on the local blacktop when the best players came to play. He was aware enough to be at bliss with that reality.

Not until his second summer of internship did Jimmy accept Jerry's summons to his local court. He had been warned by Hal and Tyrone this was no neighborhood to be caught in without the proper credentials and Jimmy had avoided the invite until he had run out of excuses, but after a couple of weeks of Jerry's persistence he could no longer fabricate any more. Chicago is riddled with places like the neighborhood Jerry lived in. Deserted looking streets filled with people in nooks and crannies; majestic looking buildings left to decay decades before, but still occupied; piles of rubble formed by broken bricks and shards of glass; and across the street from the high rise a concrete park, with chain link fences half rusted and metal backboards mounted on metal poles, with thick chain link nets that made a chinging sound when the ball clanged against what was truly the iron.

There were too many bodies competing for too small a space for a game of Twenty-One not to break out. After enduring all the hard stares and a few subtle chin lifts of acceptance, all made possible by Jerry's endorsement, Jimmy entered the fray with the sole purpose of working on his rejection timing. Sometimes when he walked on a strange court in a foreign circumstance Jimmy would take advantage of the fact no one knew his game and he would change it to suite a spontaneous fantasy that in his imagination the landscape afforded. This day he saw himself as Bill Russell, able to block every shot taken in the lane, as no one in the crowd of twenty odd players mulling around the basket waiting for the next shot to bounce off the rim was over six two. Like Russell, he didn't bother with trying to chase down any of the jumpers he tossed back, he left that to the minions scurrying around him. Instead he waited for the next attempt to invade his territory, begging for it with his posture. Come on down here and get some, boys, there's plenty left.

When the Deuce and a Quarter pulled up, the chrome shinier than the sun it was reflecting, custom green paint speckled with sparkles covering the rest, Jimmy had just rejected number eight, and it had become somewhat of a game inside the game amongst the others - who can take this tall stranger to the basket and sneak the ball past him? Settling for a jump shot became an act of cowardice. He noticed the young man stepping out of the driver's seat, muscles rippling under his ribbed, sleeveless undershirt, and his three companions, tall, large and silent types, there because he was there, not dressed to play. When he stepped onto the court the others parted like the spectators on a mountain stage of the Tour de France.

But then the game began resumed. Twenty-One is a game you can jump in the middle of, no questions asked, other than the score if you are really trying to win. Jimmy kept his spot a step in front of the basket waiting for his next victim, the next fly to march into the pitcher plant, and when the ball came to Mr. 225 he took it straight at him, leaping with the power and grace of a superior athlete, and then, as Jimmy leapt to meet him, eyes bulging as they zoomed in on the target, he switched hands, ducked under, and extended his right hand to release the ball. Damn, thought Jimmy, as he swatted helplessly at the spinning orb, this was a move he himself could be proud of, but then he noticed his conqueror was holding the ball a fraction longer than necessary, to admire his artistry just a bit more. Jimmy reached a little farther, but the ball easily slipped by, bounced gracefully off the backboard, and dropped through the rim.

"Not today, home boy!" Mr. 225 howled as he walked to the line for his free throws.

Jimmy smiled back, and meant it. This guy had some moves, that was for sure, and had some hops to go along as a tasty side dish. A full meal for the taking. He dropped all three free throws, not leaving any doubt about each as they left his hand, and took the ball at the key. As a measure of respect, and to make sure the rest of the crowd got the message, Jimmy walked from his established perch and stopped at the free throw line to greet him.

With a quick jab step left he blew by Jimmy to the right, starting his course down the lane against the less than committed group standing there. Jimmy peeled around and sped down the lane as well, a half step behind but a half thought ahead, and leapt when he saw his adversary leap, too far out of reach to stop, but not if he kept to the pattern dictated by his ego. Yes, thought Jimmy as 225 suspended himself in midair for that fraction necessary for the memory of it to be embedded in the minds of those with the privilege of witnessing, and he reached out to meet the ball as it was released into the air, tapping it gently to alter it from its sure destination inside the net to a harmless carom off the backboard and back into the hands of its previous owner.

With surprise and anger he caught his rejected offering and with extreme care and a prudent fade away banked it in over all the outstretched arms. Three more free throws, three more splashes, and one long hard stare at Jimmy later, Mr. 225 was at the key again, staring down Jimmy with absolute resolution. To change it up he went left this time, using another as a screen, but instead of taking the open jumper he could have made with very little difficulty, he had to take it to the hole. Having his shot blocked had to be erased in the minds of those around him, and in his own mind especially, and it had to happen immediately. He was first to the baseline, along the left side of the basket, and he took a strong step with his right foot down the line before anyone could stop him. Jimmy had seen this move, had accomplished this move, and had seen it done by the master, George Gervin, so many times he was critiquing it as he watched it unfold. To make it work against real shot blockers the shooter must leave the ground with options, and not be fixed on one outcome, or he was in extreme danger of getting snuffed. The basics were using either hand or even better either side of the rim, and masters like George had eight variations of each. Mr. 225, as Jimmy had previously observed, was all right handed, was used to being quicker than everyone he couldn't out-jump and did not have the imagination to overcome those deficiencies. The quickness and leaping ability were what got him into trouble. Once in the air he could see Jimmy soaring down the lane to greet him, still rising as he reached the peak of his jump, and despite sticking his butt out and leaning forward to block Jimmy's progress, he could do nothing other than release the ball and hope it would make it to the backboard without being altered.

It didn't. Jimmy turned his body in mid-air to avoid him and was arcing back to Earth as he caught the ball, in true Russell fashion, in one hand and slammed it against the backboard and pressed it there for the fraction of time it took the rest of his body to catch up and slid it down as he landed on both feet with the ball in his hand. Yes, in honor of Mr. Russell, he had cleaned the glass. Then he took it straight up and laid it against the board and dropped it in.

I've always written about you.
Even when I was so small I didn't know the language;
The meaning never changed.
I rocked, I ran, and tumbled with words
Which all spelled out neatly when re-arranged:
The hostage writes for fear of captivity,
A ransom note for my heart.

Saw a mile of fantasy in your eyes.
It took a touch from my core,
And sent me back to the beginnings of desire.
Found a gut level melody that described a rhythm
Which translated life into liquid –
Winked a tear from the corner of my smile.

You wish to know how the seasons remain,
How the Earth pushes living pillars through its surface.
My pen understands as it scrawls out its message,
As it deciphers the tangled web of my questions,
It has wiggled for you all along.

A few years later Jimmy found out who it was that he had rejected. It was at Jerry's wedding reception, of all places. Jimmy was sitting at the bar, with a drink in his hand listening to the music and watching the happy couple dance, when a man next to him, someone Jimmy had never met before, began to tremble in fear.

"Aw man," he said as he watched a group enter the room. "It's Lucky Carlos. What's he doin' here?"

Jimmy looked over and saw a familiar face, but couldn't pinpoint it, but from the look on Lucky's face, he could pinpoint Jimmy. He was wearing the kind of suit Mafia guys would wear to church, if the Mafia had been founded in Louisiana by Creoles. As he walked toward him, Jimmy realized where he'd seen the three big guys before, and they had the same looks on their faces they had after Jimmy had wiped the glass with their boss's layup, like they were ready to kick his ass at the snap of a finger. Somehow, when he was on the court that day, those looks had been funny. Today, not so much.

"Who is he?" Jimmy asked, out of the corner of his mouth, since Lucky was halfway across the room and striding closer every second.

"He runs the 'hood. Been runnin' it for years. You know, the P-Stone Gangster set."

Before Jimmy could decide how to play it the man was standing in front of him, looking down at him sternly. Jimmy didn't get up.

"I know you," said Lucky, leaning over to stick his finger deeply into Jimmy's chest. His three cohorts were standing in a semi-circle surrounding Jimmy, and the folks sitting on either barstool suddenly needed to use the restroom or get a drink or get on the dance floor - but had an urgent reason of some kind or another to leave the stools on either side available. The big guys didn't take them.

Jimmy's response was a half-smile and a half tilt of his head in recognition, more frozen than cool, even though to those observing it may have seemed cool.

"You got that left hand," continued the owner of the finger digging into Jimmy's ribs.

"Yeah, that's me," said Jimmy, no longer able to act innocent.

"Nobody blocks my shot like that, man," Lucky Carlos growled, and then he hesitated, as if waiting for Jimmy to apologize, to show him the respect he constantly demanded, but even men who wield the power of life and death over others with the flick of their wrist respect true love, and if an approbation had escaped from Jimmy's mouth it would have exposed him as a pretender. When Jimmy shrugged but said nothing, made no attempt to acquiesce to the power standing in front of him, Lucky Carlos knew this was a man he could honor.

Lucky smiled, and from past experiences Jimmy knew that could be a good or bad omen, but when the three men surrounding them eased their postures it was the sign to all the onlookers, including the one with the most at stake, things would not end with blood on the floor. Of course Jimmy couldn't keep his tongue still.

"Don't worry, man," he said returning the smile, "I do that to everybody."

Lucky was turning to leave as those words tumbled out, and they caused his torso to involuntarily lock at the sound of them. Lucky turned back, his smile still calm but more than a few degrees chillier, then he diverted his eyes to the bartender and said, "Get me a shot of Remy, and get my man here whatever he's havin'." And then he slapped Jimmy on the back and snarled out, "Come on down to my spot again soon man, and I'll be waitin' for ya'."

When Lucky Carlos turned and walked away after downing his glass, it was the last time Jimmy saw him in life. He made sure of it by never going anywhere near that court again.

Another boring Ethics class had brought that memory back vividly, the words spoken so many months before were fresher in Jimmy's mind than what Doctor Pickard had said in the last minute. Something about space travel. He had asked the class what they thought of it, from the moral perspective, and there was near universal acclamation that space travel, finding new worlds to exploit and conquer, was not only important, it was essential to the advancement, no, to the survival of the human species. There was only so much oil here, only a small amount of precious metals, a limited amount of air to breathe and the amount of time the industrial world would allow it to be breathable was finite as well. That's why they were all here, to help make that bright future a reality in whatever measure they could, small as their reality or as big as their dreams.

After letting his charges wax on for fifteen minutes, extolling the bright future we had to look forward to in the vacuum of the universe, Dr. Pickard asked the following question.

"So, no one thinks the money we spend on the space program could be better spent helping people who are starving here on Earth, right now?"

The groan from the congregation was louder than when their esteemed instructor surprised them with a pop quiz. Even thinking about such a question offended the political, intellectual, and patriotic morality that had guided and nurtured this group to this point in their lives.

"Every dollar spent on the space program helps poor people more than giving them handouts!" shouted out Cory Black, sure this time he would not be shot down by his classmates, the ones it mattered to him not getting shot down by anyway.

When Jimmy laughed in derision, knowing he would be the only one doing so, Cory was not disappointed. Frank Torres had his back.

"Give a man a fish and he'll eat for a day. Teach a man to fish and he'll eat forever. As long as we keep giving people free fish they will always be poor."

Jimmy knew he should keep quiet, that he should save his breath for more fruitful activities, but he just couldn't.

"As long as you don't dam the river and then pollute the lake. Go back in time far enough and you'll find that guy's great, great, great grandfather taught yours how to fish in the first place, then your great, great, grandfather took away his right to fish where he'd been fishing for centuries."

As was normal in this class when he spoke up this way, Jimmy was met with silence. No argument followed, since Jimmy could not be expected to think about American culture and history clearly, he didn't have to be taken seriously by the other students, and Dr. Pickard knew he didn't have anything to teach him, only the others.

Ian needed to bring the discussion back to the majority's comfort zone, and in his standard measured tones which demanded silent contemplation opined, "The current hardships suffered by the few will eventually be swept away by the progress the space program and the many technologies that are coming out of it will bring us. To stop it would be a victory of ignorance and pessimism over prosperity and optimism."

"Shouldn't we learn to live together here before we spread our violence and greed to other planets?" asked the good doctor to his favorite patient.

Cory had the last word, spoken the second before the ringing of the bell which ended every debate, no matter how heated.

"Well, we can't let the commies get there first, no matter what!"

12. Seventeen New Positions #7

The tenth of March technically falls into the band of time designated as winter, and in Illinois the air can remain so cold snow and ice survive in the shadows of the sparse heat of the low hung sun, but the turn of the calendar to the month when spring begins brings the warmth of it into the hearts of all who meagerly survive until the days are longer than the nights. So it was with the glow from the beams of this imagined sunlight warming his soul Jimmy climbed aboard the commuter flight from Peoria Airport to O'Hare Airport, Chicago, to go to an interview set up by a recruiter from Continental Container Company, a business Jimmy had no real knowledge of and not much curiosity about. The only reason he had agreed was the recruiter on the other end of the line was so persistent, and the man he talked to from American had bragged so much about not being worried if he talked to other companies because they wouldn't offer as much.

Peoria had the kind of small city airport that evoked the era of black and white movies, and the planes operating out of it fit that role as well. Passengers walked from the terminal building onto the tarmac carrying their luggage and handed it to porters next to the belly of the plane before walking up the steps and into the fuselage. Jimmy had flown before, but never on a plane so small he had to bend at the waist to walk down the narrow aisle, but at least all the seats were window seats. He had no bags, no briefcase, only a notebook with his ticket stuffed inside and the mechanical pencil he had taken from the desk during his last summer's internship. He didn't need anything more, as the plan was for the recruiter, a man named Tom Ford, to meet him at the terminal and drive him to the office from there. His return flight was late in the afternoon, scheduled such that Jimmy would have time upon his arrival to return to campus before the cafeteria closed. Once everyone had found their seats the pilot cranked the props and rolled down the runway and was soon flying over the cornfields and soy bean fields and wheat fields, rolling rectangles broken only by the dirt roads and an occasional gently winding river, until the flashing lights of the runway guided him to his destination.

Upon landing at the airport Jimmy was not met by Tom Ford. The terminal was such a bustling place with so many people rushing in so many directions Jimmy couldn't fathom finding someone he knew, and when Tom Ford wasn't standing there waiting for him he didn't know what to do next but to sit by the gate and wait. After waiting for half an hour - his initial plan was an hour, but his youth wouldn't allow such patience - he wandered through the terminal looking for someone who looked to be looking for him, but soon realized the futility of that approach and returned to the gate and sat there, trying to be vigilant.

Being a point guard was never something Jimmy desired to be until he saw the NCAA Tournament in 1979. It was the tourney that started the greatest rivalry ever seen between equal and opposite warriors in any sport and was the turning point on which the style of the game played in the 70's was eclipsed by the styles of the 80's and beyond, the styles of Larry Bird and Magic Johnson. The final game was highly anticipated by fans everywhere, as Magic Johnson was the most talked about freshman to ever play college ball and Larry Bird was a legend as a senior and the greatest player Jimmy had ever seen play in person, the year before against Illinois State.

That year Indiana State was an above average team that happened to have the best college player in the nation on it, while Illinois State was hovering near the top twenty for the first time in its history. The game was highly anticipated, and so much gossip had been spread about this Bird guy Sonny picked up Jimmy from his dorm in Peoria and drove to Normal to meet up with Jimmy's sister. She was a senior at Illinois State and had the tickets. They sat in the student section and watched in awe the best game Jimmy had ever seen in person, and maybe ever would.

The Illinois State Redbirds were led by a forward named Billy Lewis who scored a little over 20 points a game. He was talented enough to be drafted, but not to make an NBA roster, and not nearly skilled enough to guard Bird, also a forward, who averaged an ungodly 30 points a game and 11.5 rebounds. The Redbirds tried about everything to stop Bird, double teams, box and one zones, full court presses, but what got everyone's attention was when the Redbirds switched to a half court zone trap. The trap is sprung when the ball is passed into one of the four corners of the half court and two defenders corner the man with the ball, forcing a bad pass or a strip of the ball. When they trapped Bird, standing at least 30 feet from the basket if not 35 feet, he calmly rose for a picture-perfect jump shot, all six foot nine of him, and drilled it without rippling the net. This was the kind of desperation shot other great, and I mean all-time great, shooters would only try at the end of the half or game, and Bird made it look pedestrian. No one watching believed it was more than a lucky shot, and some of the Redbird fans let Larry know it as he trotted back on defense. That was why the next time down the court he drifted to the same spot, took a step farther away, and drained another jumper. It had to be 35 feet at least, and he stared at Gene Smithson on the Redbird bench instead of watching the ball in flight, to let him know the half-court trap was to his liking so Gene could keep playing it as long as he liked. Gene called time out and tried something else just as futile, but at least Larry was dropping normal shots from then on. The game did not end before overtime, during which there was an epic brawl, and the Redbirds pulled it out and went on to win the conference title.

The next year was Bird's last, and Coach Hodges brought in the kind of transfer players the Great One needed to win every game of the year until the National Final. There were see-saw victories along the way against great squads from Arkansas and DePaul with a winning margin of only a basket, but Bird and his mates were still unblemished as they took the court against Michigan State, the Number 2 team with the Number 2 player, an otherworldly talented eighteen year old who played point guard at six foot eight, which all the experts thought was impossible until they saw it, just like Bird's skills were not to be believed until witnessed. To put it bluntly, Larry Bird was not only a phenomenal scorer and prolific rebounder, he was by far the best and most creative passer ever to play forward or center in the history of basketball. And Magic was the best passer to play the sport who ever lived at any position in any era.

The two could not have been more opposite. Larry was first and foremost a scorer and scored thirty without much exertion, but he would pass and rebound or do whatever else it took to win. He was the leading scorer, rebounder and assist man on the team. Magic could have scored 30 points a game any night he wanted to, but he didn't want to, he'd rather have at least 10 rebounds and 10 assists to go along with the points he straggled together, always more than 10 as well. Throw in a few steals and he would really start to feel motivated. Larry played with a snarl, distaining his opponents with a constant stream of trash talk everyone quickly learned was not bragging, as he did exactly what he said he was going to do, and no one could stop him. Magic played with a smile that could blind a sun worshipper and would laugh and hug the hapless players sent to do battle with him, letting them know he loved them almost as much as the players wearing the same uniform as he did. At first it was hard to tell if it was real or posturing, but before the game was over you knew there was nothing phony about the man child's charm.

By the time the final game was played, both had established themselves as the new stars of the new decade, despite the game itself not being that close. Magic won, proving to Jimmy being the best passer trumped being the best shooter, playing faster did not mean playing more selfishly, and the best ego stroke was to win, not to be the highest scorer, and a beautiful pass could be just as poetic, dramatic, and rewarding as a slam dunk.

His stomach was growling as he sat in the softly uncomfortable seat in the terminal, still no Tom Ford in sight and no other options having occurred. He looked at his return flight ticket and saw in it a vision of his future. Oh, the places he would go!

Indiana was full of Larry Birds, despite none of the others being even remotely as talented and almost none being as tall. He couldn't have come from anywhere else. Whether they be six foot six or five foot six, they all carried the same tool box. They played rough, shot well, were aware of the classic tactics of the game known as the "fundamentals", whether they strictly adhered to them or not - and most of them did - and first and foremost, were mouthy as hell. Most, like Larry, needed a tan, as the only exercise they got was indoors, with white pasty complexions usually adorned with pimples sticking out of their tight shorts and tank tops, but that didn't hinder them from a constant stream of profanity laced vitriol on the court as they proclaimed to their opponents and teammates and spectators and passersby the game would end in their favor.

Jimmy was twenty-four years old, more than two years past his college graduation and working at American Oil. It was the prime of his bachelor life, the era when money flowed in faster than it left and no debts accumulated, when parties did not have to end before the sun came up and often didn't, when women were trifles to be sampled and tossed aside, when hangovers sometimes didn't have the chance to start before the next workday began, and he could still indulge in his greatest passion on at least one weeknight and again on the weekend, still able to give it the sweaty devotion needed to keep the magic flowing for a little while longer.

But he knew it was nearly finished. He had seen her openly flirting with mere boys, not even bothering to hide it, in his face. There was so little time before he drifted away from her, or was forced out, every opportunity had to be taken to indulge in her, to let her know he hadn't forgotten her among the other earthly delights at his disposal in the darkly bright city he now called home. But he could never be monogamous again, and had to admit he always knew she never had been, despite his delusions of her chastity.

So as he walked down the court it struck him of all the games he had played, of all the times he had stepped onto a basketball court and fought for his honor, he had never been in this exact situation before. He was humbled, at this point, to be able to have the chance at one last glory, at one last time to have it proven to him that yes, he was loved, if only for an instant of time.

He was playing in a rec league in Hammond, Indiana, for adults twenty-one and over. It was the typical crowd of twenty and thirty something ballers, trying to get the last bites of their athletic apples just like Jimmy. In a few years they would be transferring their primitive urges to dominate to their sons' little league careers, but for now they were letting them loose on the court. Jimmy was playing on a team a guy at work had put together from their work league team and was willing to drive the thirty miles to get in some run.

The game, as all games in this league, was rough, and no open layups were allowed unless the defenders were too tired or slow to place a forearm or knee in the path of the driver. It came down to the last twenty seconds, and Jimmy's team, the Gremlins, were down by one, thirty-six to thirty-five, and had the ball and called a time out. There was just enough time for the point guard, and Jimmy was playing the point, to take the ball down the lane and dish it to one of the big guys who would then go up strong for the basket, leaving them time for a rebound and another chance if the first shot was missed.

Their opponents, however, didn't let this plan unfold. Their point guard, all five foot eight of him, in his mid-thirties and no longer svelte, but still hanging on with all his appendages to his favorite toy, tried to steal the ball from Jimmy as he made his drive. Jimmy turned and put his shoulder between his man and the ball and the resulting collision brought on the screech of the official's whistle, despite the shorter man having managed to swipe away the ball.

"What???" screamed Little Larry, the man who had been targeted. "That was a goddamned clean fucking steal!!!!"

Jimmy laughed in response, and rolled his eyes. Little Larry hadn't stopped talking since they were standing around the circle for the opening tipoff, so it was no surprise what came out of his mouth. No one, not even Little Larry himself, believed the steal was clean, but that only meant he had to protest even more vehemently to convince himself it was.

Time out was called again, to give Jimmy's arms time to shrink before he started his stroll toward the basket, to give him time to contemplate long and hard about the pressure he was under. He had one and one free throws, which meant he had to make the first to tie the game and get the second, and if he did he could take the second to win the game. The most pressure packed shots a player, at any level, can be tasked with making, with the game totally dependent on the outcome of each, especially the first. She had never given him this terrible delight before, and he suspected it was because there were none younger for her to bestow such a gift on in this gym this night, but he thanked her for giving him the challenge and took it on as one more chance, maybe one of his last chances, he could never know, to prove to her how worthy of her love he remained.

"You fucking got fucking ripped," Little Larry was chirping at him from the time the huddle broke. "You fucking know you fucking don't even fucking deserve to take these fucking free throws you are fucking about to fucking miss." He was walking along side Jimmy, accompanying him as he strode to the free throw line. "The fucking steal was fucking clean and you fucking know it. Just fucking admit it."

By now Jimmy had reached the line, but the chatter did not stop.

"The goddamned ref was just fucking trying to help your shitty asses out, 'cause no way you motherfuckers can beat us without them cocksuckers helping you."

It was like music to his ears. The harsh words had the opposite effect on Jimmy than was intended. They cleared his mind and reminded him of why he had fallen in love so deeply instead of damaging his psyche and deterring his aim. He was free to fail and free to succeed in his next endeavor. No one could determine the outcome but him. The ref would toss him the ball, he would toe the line, and use all the repetitious movements he had been mastering for all these many years to allow Newton's laws to act on the orb he launched into flight and send it to its destiny. All his tormentor could do was watch.

Three Pointers

Poetry is a pack of lies
Lonely people tell themselves,
Articulate time bombs that
Explode in the reader's mind,
If the poet has a detonator
Or lights the fuse.

Engineering is based on
Unchangeable facts.
The details becoming more and more delicate
From their beginnings as
Broad brush physics,
As abstract mathematics.
The details swarm you, envelope
you, anesthetize you.
All the problems, solved and unsolved,
Become one big lump of details.

They all have numbers attached:
Measurements, lengths, diameters,
Due dates, price tags, tolerances.
Numbers helpless to change themselves.

I walked in on a Monday morning,
With no hours of sleep and two hours
Of jet lag, to quit
The best job I ever had,
To give up numbers
For lies.
As if I could cheat
The end of summer
And live life like a novel.

The first free throw fell. The sag in his body as the shot dropped through the net after the ball bounced off the back, then front of the rim, even though it was falling through with the second touch and left little doubt in the eyes of those watching the outcome, belied the fact Jimmy was more relieved than pleased it had dropped in. But why had he doubted her? The game was tied, and he was much too tired for overtime. He looked at his teammates and their body language exhibited the same lack of enthusiasm as his. Little Larry stopped chattering. He knew he would need every breath if the clock was set back to 5 minutes, even though he was hoping it would, so he silently seethed deeply as the ball was again handed to Jimmy. His next effort was filled with the confident assurance only housed in souls infused with indulgent love, and it whistled through the net spinning so tightly it hesitated for an instant as if it was too proud to obey gravity before settling through the last strands and trickling out like a drop of water from a leaking faucet. Game over.

"That's lame!!" shouted Tom Ford as Jimmy spoke to him over the phone from his dorm room. After waiting for hours in the terminal, Jimmy found the gate from which his return flight departed and boarded it. He hadn't been back in his room for five minutes when the phone rang.

"I waited for you where you said to meet you," said Jimmy meekly in response to Tom Ford's harshness.

"We are looking for people with initiative!!" shouted the recruiter. "Why didn't you just get in a cab and come to the office yourself?"

"We can try again," offered Jimmy. Money for a cab ride across Chicago had not been in his wallet, so that hadn't been an option. He felt no need to explain.

"Hah!! No way!! We don't want you!!" Tom Ford shouted, then hung up before he wasted any more of his time.

And with that Jimmy's interviewing process ended. He would go to work for American Oil, and not waste any more time with looking for a job since he already had one. He had presentations to give, games to win, and poems to gift. That should be enough to keep him occupied until the May flowers blossomed to set him free.

13. Self-Explanatory

He was an artist.
His job was to make complicated things simple,
To make the simple complex.
He borrowed much from others like him,
Adding style and filling spaces with odds and ends of ideas.

Others enjoyed the way he thought –
Content was secondary.
He rode on in contempt of his unasked-for ability –
In fear of losing it;
Of blindness in the contemporary talent watchers –
While knowing all possessed his own store.

His mind had been sent to the wilderness
To purge it of childishness;
The rain of loneliness to wash it away,
To step from the cocoon into manhood
With no need to look back, or falter in indecision –
The wild would show him his master, and the call.

He felt his heart pushing blood through his veins,
Knowing it would be finite;
He knew the meaning and reason for joy
And he lived to translate it to his sons and daughters.

He was an artist.

About a block and a half from Jimmy's childhood home was the old two-story brick school in which he attended first, second, and third grade. It closed a couple of years later and the remainder of the glass windows not broken during the neighborhood boys' target practice were boarded up. For a few more years the blacktop where he spent many a frigid and sweltering recess, chasing and being chased, dodging balls and clutching at pigtails, was still intact, with only a few weeds forcing their way through the cracks slowly tearing open the asphalt. There was one bent hoop with an old semi-circular backboard and no net at one end, and it was Jimmy's home court from the time he outgrew the hoop in his driveway until he reached the age when they let him play inside.

Once his desire had been ignited in the fifth grade it did not matter if the opponents were real or invisible or whether it was hot or cold, when the urge struck he would take the best ball he had and frolic in his sanctuary. As the years passed his preference to go when he knew no others would be present grew, as all the best games he played there were imaginary anyway. It was then he could play a whole game right handed if the urge struck him, he was always the one to take the last shot, he could play center and take slow sweeping hook shots or be the mosquito who only shot from long range. No one could complain if he decided to shoot nothing but twisting, turning, impossibilities; to conjure releases and spins to gauge if they sprang or faded after kissing the backboard, to learn to coax the ball into caressing the rim, to roll along it and around it before falling through, to develop the softness of a master. And in those games the buzzer miraculously did not sound after his last second flick bounced away instead of through the rim. There was always a chance for a rebound and put back, or a tip in.

But more than fantasies were played out on that stretch of blacktop. Countless hours were spent silently repeating the drills he had been learning since his first practice. Dribbling right handed down the blacktop and back, as fast as he could, then left handed, then left to right to left, then spinning right and left, then, as the years passed, and skills grew, between the legs and behind the back. Layup after layup, left handed, right handed, angling across with either hand, again and again. Jump shots from the classic spots: baseline, free throw line extended, top of the key, first direct and then banked. Big man moves from either block with all their countless variations. Bank shots twisting, stopping after a dead run, one handed. Repeated until the clouds burst open or the sun tired and fell behind the horizon, or his mother's voice wailed out for him to return for a meal, and ending, when exhaustion came, and the light was fading, with free throws. Ten, then twenty, then fifty, then a hundred as his stamina and freedom increased.

At no time did he need this piece of heaven more than on the day he was told he was no longer welcome in the varsity basketball gymnasium. In his junior year of high school the final fifteen didn't include him. He had never had to absorb such a crushing blow, to be given such a denouncement of his talents and desires, but in the lives of the truly passionate defeats and slights are sacred blessings sent to strengthen them. They are the tests that qualify and cleanse the righteous through their suffering. The moment when the rock stops rolling and is at the bottom of the hill, after having spent so much time and effort to push it as far up as he had, would he walk away or put his shoulder back into it, and start heaving and straining again? Without having answered that question, no lover deserves his beloved.

And so every day the weather would allow he came to worship. First to ask, 'why me?', then to work on the things he had been accused of weakness in, then for the pure joy of it. He loved this game. He would play it under any circumstances he could. Everyone he played against again would have to be made to marvel at how he could ever have been cut from any small town high school team. Those who were picked over him would have to be made to admit it was unjust. But most of all, he was consumed with raising his skill level to the point they had to let him play whenever he walked into any gym and someone else could sit by and watch and enjoy the show, not him, and when it was over he was the one they would be talking about.

How he started was how he started, literally. The first poem he ever wrote, The Sweetness, was the first one he slipped under a door, to his first and favorite muse, Talia Simone. The fear of exposure, so loud it was squealing like the brakes of a subway train in his mind as he walked down the hall, was balanced by his calmly knowing he could not be possibly suspected. He had been so loudly quiet in the social scene on campus for four years, not one to flirt or openly pursue any one of the many who were available, so seemingly intent on his studies and his private and public passions the girls had given up on him. They all knew who he was, of course, so he was a known mystery, but when the growing roster of recipients created their list of suspects he was not even mentioned, let alone deemed worthy of the top ten, and the pursuit of the culprit never even got warm.

There was Debra Martin, Talia's best friend willing to bear the tragically poetic reality of being treated as the second best looking wherever they went, and little Ann Marquis, so petite and well endowed, sunny most days but quick to gather storm clouds on others, and Jenny Adams, moody, brilliant and beautiful, who Jimmy had actually tried to talk to a couple of times, really just once with the second a close to term abortion after he had started to pour out his feelings, caused by Jenny's declaration of her heart belonging to someone she proudly declared did not deserve it. Paul Carpenter's older sister Patricia, curly blond hair and all, got It Is Immortal, since he had written it for her. Long before he had met Paul, Jimmy had shared a study room with her for a half hour before her boyfriend whisked her away. If it wasn't for Paul, Jimmy wouldn't have ever known her name.

It was not a haphazard operation, this stealthy distributing of verse to his quarry. First, he had to determine from his many stacks of notebooks which poems were worthy of releasing. Then he had to match them with the target audience. If a poem had been written for a specific person he tried to give it to that person, but if he hadn't had someone specific in mind at the time he was writing it sometimes he did after and made that his criteria, and some he gave because he wanted to impress and thought what he was sending was impressive. He kept no records of whom he was sending them to, only which ones he was sending, thereby making sure each was only sent once. Somehow, he thought it less incriminating if his room was searched and no such list was found, despite the poems themselves being stacked in his closet. But the hardest part was finding out which doors to slip his neatly tri-folded sheets of paper under and which mailboxes to stuff and finding the perfect time to do it. He found himself walking down the halls of dorms he had not traversed in the eight semesters he had lived on this campus in the darkness, his hood up and hands stuffed in his pockets like a thief escaping with his pilfered bounty. By the end of the project he was quite the ninja; blending in, completing his errand and escaping into the darkness, not leaving a whisper or a fiber or a scent to be traced, each getaway a unique but familiarly thrilling climax.

14. Lyrics

It wasn't enough for Jimmy to play in one league in his final semester. Sonny called him the first week back on campus and begged him to join his Y league team in Canton as well, and after at first refusing, Jimmy had a strong bout of nostalgia and couldn't pass up the opportunity to play with his childhood friends again, one last time; Bob and Chance and Sonny and Jimmy, with only Watay missing to complete the old high school quintet. Jimmy's practical reason for not agreeing, which has been explained already, was he was not a member of the Y and couldn't afford to join it, but Sonny agreed to pay for it, as he was flush for the few more months of freedom he had left before the profits of his business turned into legal fees. With more faith in his old Oldsmobile than its current level of reliability deserved, Jimmy made the thirty-mile trek once a week, sometimes stopping by his parents' house to eat, sometimes not, and proudly walked to the desk and checked in and received a locker key. Not even a month had passed since they had escorted him out in January.

Two types of teams played in the Y league in Canton. There were the ones like Sonny had formed, of guys in their early twenties not concerned with staying in shape, but to have fun playing and showing off; and those of older guys who were trying to hang on and keep the past glory of their high school team alive as long as possible. The games between young teams were not very serious, and artistic maneuvers were encouraged and the outcomes not so dire, but the games between young teams and older teams were always intense. They were never sophisticated, poetically gentile affairs. Normally they were coarse, irritable bouts of passion more sadistic than artistic, in which rapidly atrophying men vainly reached for the last morsels of their lives' athletic glory in increasingly cynical ways. Someday, and not a long day off, Jimmy would be one of them, but for now he looked on such men with a dearth of pity and a glut of scorn, like they were ex-boyfriends not willing to accept the reality of the girl being his now.

In the very first game of the year for the 365er's the horn didn't have enough time to blow signaling the end of the half before a brawl was a nose away from erupting. That nose belonged to a thirty something man, with a paunch and a bald spot, slightly shorter than Jimmy to give him a good view of it. The guy should have known better, but he was so loaded with machismo the fact the forearm Bob landed on his noggin was accidental did not allow that. It wasn't as if it was the first elbow thrown under the basket in the game and Bob hadn't received more than he'd given, but there was no time left for backing down in the older man's mind. The referee stepped in - before Sonny decided he'd be the one to bring blood from that nose if Bob wasn't - and let both sides know they could either calm down or take it outside, but the cheap shots had to stop.

Jimmy knew exactly how to stop it. He had adapted to the circumstances surrounding him on this team by playing forward, his position in high school, a position that had long since outgrown him, because in this league that was what was needed. So instead of bringing the ball up court as the point guard, he was waiting at the free throw line, his back to the basket, his arm up asking for the pass from Sonny, and for some reason, maybe fate intervening, Sonny agreed to pass it. When he felt the slight push in his back as he caught the pass he knew who was guarding him before he turned, and now was the time to change this game. Spinning on his left foot, he encountered the glaring face he expected - spittle in the corners of the mouth waiting to turn into foam - and made his move, a quick jab step to his right with his right leg, then a strong step forward to his left with his right foot, taking a swift but deliberate dribble. He could out quick this guy to the hole and not be much bothered, but that was not his intent. His defender saw what he thought was coming and reacted by lunging to his right, to meet Jimmy at the basket, not to block the shot, but to explode into the shooter. Instead of going around him as his defender expected, Jimmy lowered his shoulder and pushed hard off his left foot, directly into the chest of the man, taking full advantage of the laws of motion to amplify the impact and launch him down the lane sliding on his backside out of bounds. No sound was heard except the whistle, not even the squeak of a shoe, and the referee pointed to the man crumpled under the basket trying to re-expand his lungs, and shouted, "That's a foul! Two shots!!"

Three Pointers

I.

Dear mister master
Please tell me what's the matter
My heart keeps churning faster
The truth is not found in your chatter
Come see the ashes and the tears.

II.

Rasta man
Chained in a garden of wild discontent
Freed when the last of the fortune's spent
All you need is a wild flower to keep you content
Inside the dome of consciousness
Concentrate.

III.

He thought his thought had concentrated
It was a section of his mind not abated
When he loved and schemed and hated
All was a portion which scrambled and complicated
What was struggling to be freed.

IV.

The idea wiggled and squirmed
Encountered the maze of bureaucracy
Amounting to a smokescreen.
Once the final product reached the consumer
It was too involved for a short story.

Even though he knew he was truly blessed with love, Jimmy was under no illusion it was because he was handsome or in any way attractive to the eye. There was no reason for anyone, even Jimmy looking at himself in a mirror, to suspect he was as deeply loved as he was by the body in which he was ensconced. It was not uncommon for other males to try to use him to impress the ladies, to show their dominance over the weak and fearfully unloved as he surely appeared to be, but if they had the bad luck to try it with a basketball in their hands, not on the floor wrestling like they did when he was in grade school, someone did end up embarrassed, but it was never Jimmy. Over the course of many years Jimmy knew the next challenge could come anywhere, anytime, as he had been the one sought out so often by those looking for an easy target it was something he had learned to always be prepared for.

He had family in Peoria, and one fine day in his first year of college he was invited to dinner by his aunt, and free home cooked food was not something Jimmy would pass on, even if it meant sitting around afterwards talking and listening to his elders. He did have a female cousin named Aileen who was a year behind him in school, which was crucial because it meant she was still in high school, and she was one of those girls all the jocks gravitated toward. In fact, one of those jocks, a star on one of the local high school powers, stopped by for a wooing visit as the plates were cleared. Once he saw Jimmy sitting there innocently at the table behind his thick glasses, he felt he had found the perfect vehicle with which to show Aileen how well he could drive.

In the back yard of his uncle's house was a square of concrete with a hoop at one end, installed before his relatives moved in, that was for sure. It could not have been twenty feet by twenty feet, maybe more like fifteen, and Jimmy tried to recall if he had ever seen anyone playing on it before now, as he stood there with a full stomach in suede topped shoes with rubber bottoms, not made to play ball in, against a high school star in proper gear, one on one, with a favorite cousin there to witness. Aileen stood off to the side, hand on her hip, smiling. He had a quick impulse to refuse the challenge and return into the house, but this kid was acting like he was preparing a demonstration and Jimmy was the subject about to be hypnotized for his cousin's entertainment, and Jimmy's back stiffened.

As so many guys including Jimmy in that era knew, the girls were not impressed by jump shots. They wanted Julius Erving. They wanted high flying acrobatics. They wanted sleight of hand deceptions, soaring scoops, and thunderous dunks. So instead of standing as far away as he could and using his quickness to drop bombs from a distance Jimmy could not touch, his opponent charged into the hornet's nest. He was quicker, could jump higher, and had more strength and stamina, but Jimmy was taller and had the longer arms, the ability to jump as high as he needed, and the quickness of mind on his side, plus, as so many other times in his long romance, the other guy's ego to exploit. After making a move along the baseline Jimmy couldn't quite reach, the high schooler got greedy and thought he was at a patisserie eating sweets, and on his next foray he vainly paused, to pose for his audience, at the point he should have been releasing the ball and taking advantage of the half step he had on his defender, allowing Jimmy to make him eat leather instead. That changed the dynamic of the contest, turning from a game of points into a show of machismo, and the smaller man drove in again and again, and Jimmy swatted them away again, and again, and again. Jimmy, tired and lazy after a heavy meal, not stretched, and in the tight shoes, decided he would save his energy on offense and focus on defense, and did what the other man should have done, shoot nothing but jumpers, although he wasn't able to gain any accuracy. Instead he concentrated on blocking so many of this guy's shots that win or lose he couldn't impress Aileen, and that is what happened. Jimmy blocked about twenty of the guy's shots before he made ten, but before Jimmy could make eight jumpers. The conversation after the game made the winner sound like the loser.

"Man, I ain't never got my shot blocked like that before. You can play!! You almost beat me," said his shocked foe.

"Well, I didn't have the right shoes. Next time I'll bring 'em. I usually make a lot more of those jumpers," said an unimpressed Jimmy.

15. Absence Makes

Shack was the best player on The Yard for the first three years Jimmy was on campus. People were in absolute fear of embarrassment by him on the court. When he strode past, the gym rats fell into silent whispers. His gear was never less than spotless, hems tidy, his shorts creased down the middle as if he was going sailing. Competing against him was an honor, playing with him a privilege, and watching him a delight. He reeked of dignity, and the gravity beaming from his eyes could force rising trash talk back down his opponents' throats. From the time he put on their uniform the Campus Kings had not lost a game and Shack was truly the Bradley University Campus King of Hoops.

Large Louis called an informal practice a few days before their last game of the season to "tune up before the playoffs started," and even he was surprised when almost all five of the starters, minus Darrell - who was too involved "studying" with his girlfriend - showed up. The main floor of Haussler was large enough to hold three full courts and had two sets of sliding padded walls which opened like accordions along a track in the floor to section it into thirds, so games could be played simultaneously without players or the ball roaming into an adjoining court. Unless there was an official game being played the walls were left flattened against the outer building walls, as guys who had the energy to sprint for two hours up and down the court were too lazy to pull on the handle and close them, but on this day the room was sectioned as if something official was going to happen. The nearest section, the one with bleachers used for intramural games, had the portable scoreboard in the corner and the official's table in place, but no one was sitting there as the Goodfellas crew swaggered through it to the middle section where the action was.

They were in the middle of a pickup game when the man entered; Shack, accompanied by two of his fellow Kings, and not just any two Kings, Eddie Justice and Tray Fields. It had taken Jimmy a while after he joined the Goodfellas to pick up on it, but Eddie and Tray had gone to the same high school as Hal and Darrell but were two years ahead of them, and the dynamic of them being the subservient benchwarmers while Eddie and Tray were the dominant stars had not been shaken during their college years. And not only on the court were they the alphas. Hal and Darrell came from upper class families, but Eddie and Tray were downright rich, the kind of kids who drove to school in nicer cars than Hal and Darrell's fathers owned. Darrell had cute girlfriends, but Eddie dated the homecoming queen. Hal dressed nicely, but Tray was the one who set the trends. In every way they came second, and being acknowledged by their betters was still an event, even though they seethed in resentment when it happened, especially Hal.

That is why, even though the pickup game they were contesting was not even close to being over, when Hal was summoned he immediately stopped and answered the call. The trio of Kings stood on the side, whispering amongst themselves, Shack with his hand on Tray's shoulder.

Tray trotted over to Hal on the next in-bounds and said, "The team we were supposed to play tonight forfeited. Come on over and scrimmage against us. We can use the clock and the scoreboard. We've only got an hour, so hurry up."

"What cha think, fellas?" asked Hal, turning to Jimmy and Tyrone.

"Fuck 'em, as far as I'm concerned," said Tyrone. "We're already tired, and they're fresh." He hated Eddie even more than Hal or Darrell did, as the homecoming queen also went to Bradley and flirted with him constantly, never to give him closure, letting him know he was almost as sexy and not nearly as wealthy as her boyfriend, so teasing was all he was ever going to get.

Jimmy shrugged. This was not a show of respect, to ask them to stop in the middle of a game to help a team they may eventually face in the playoffs get a workout, and probably get a beat down in the process, but he could not help but be eager to go against Shack. He had watched him many times and had gone against him a few times, the last being in the playoffs the year before with his last team, the Pyramids. Jimmy had fouled out trying to battle with the big boys inside, as he had to play forward with the Pyramids, and he vowed that would be the last game he would play that position. One of those fouls was a hard collision with Shack as they scrambled for a loose ball, and Shack was not pleased and let Jimmy know it. This would be the first chance for Shack to give him a proper response.

"Let's go," said Jimmy, more to Shack than his own teammates.

The game started with Shack dribbling up court with the partial Goodfellas squad defending. The Goodfellas point guard that year, Pete Peters, picked him up near half court. Shack responded by throwing a lazy pass to Tray, guarded by Jimmy, who feasted on lazy passes. He was so well known for it as soon as the ball left his hands Shack grabbed at the air to bring it back in vain as Jimmy stepped in front of Tray and caught the ball like it was meant to be thrown to him in the first place. From the time he stepped on a court as a small boy Jimmy considered all lazy passes to be his, because the older boys would never throw him the ball and he had to figure out ways to get it for himself, and lazy passes turned out to be some of the best opportunities. He was at full sprint after two dribbles.

Shack was known as the best defender on The Yard, not just the best player. No one would envy the position Jimmy was in now, going one on one against Shack, who everyone, especially Jimmy, watching from the court or the bleachers could see had the angle on him. The stands were speckled with people, mostly girlfriends and a few of the Kings' groupies, and they all took a deep breath as they watched the two men sprinting toward the Goodfellas' goal. They locked eyes, and Shack's glare let Jimmy know what he was thinking. He was thinking about the knot on his head from Jimmy's shoulder smashing into him the year before and the week it took for the swelling to subside. It was time to re-establish, no re-confirm, his dominance. After hastily concluding his chances of out-quicking or out-running Shack as minimal, Jimmy slowed down, which to everyone watching made it look like he was inviting Shack to catch up, something he did often to opponents who couldn't jump with him, to give them a better view of him scoring over them, but a decision he would soon regret against a supreme leaper like Shack. Shack timed his jump perfectly to intercept the ball as it was released deliberately from Jimmy's right hand. Jimmy did not bother to fake, or take a long step, or do anything to mask his intentions. He jumped off his right foot and stretched out his right arm with the ball cupped in his right hand for all to see. Once Shack left his feet Jimmy lingered in his pose for half a heartbeat, but then brought the ball back to rest against his belly button clutched by both hands. This was way, way, way, too easy. He was surprised Shack was so eager to embarrass him and was therefore this easily trapped. Shack saw this amused look as he sailed past, his hand swatting at air. Jimmy lifted his legs to bring his knees toward his chest as he rocked the baby left then right then extended the ball in his left hand and let it rotate down his digits in a balletic style. Jimmy would give full credit to George Gervin if he had been there. He finger-rolled with a flourish adorned with all the extra mustard he could relish it with, then did a little dance after the ball dropped through the net. The girlfriends gasped, trying to stifle a giggle, but the guys let out a hoop and a laugh Shack hadn't had directed his way in all the years he'd been the King of The Yard. Someone had not only stolen a pass from him, that man had then led him to the water and made him drink. Word spread around The Yard like sparks around a campfire.

Telephone call
I miss you!
The peacefulness of soul,
Fullness of spirit,
Absence of gloom - erased.
And it enters
On soft cat's feet.
Come to me
And finish the portrait.

Creepin' in through the alley door
Ain't ya?
Untouchable stuff
Two steps ahead -
A judgment call on your part.
Can't blame you.
I also detest sticky situations
And inconsiderate night dreams
Who haven't the courtesy
To leave their names.

Most, if not all, of the poems Jimmy wrote were failures, and he knew it. If he had sent them to experts in the field and they had liked them he would doubt their credentials. Why he was driven to write them he could not fathom, why he wrote them the way he did made no sense to him if he was going to write them, why he had not shown them to anyone after bleeding from his pores and tear ducts to put the words on the paper proved the insanity. But they steadily sprang forth, some so brittle he imagined they would shatter into a thousand pieces when the envelopes containing them were opened, some so liquid they would puddle on the floor if opened upside down.

There was one he named 'Ivy Covered Walls' which was not written about the unrequited passion for a woman, but about the institution he was matriculating through; a rumination on whether he was being loved and nurtured or being cynically manipulated by it. A calculation of a fashion only an engineer could fathom, to determine which element was strongest, how much of the first he could absorb without being stained by the second. He was sure by this point he was being stained, and the reason his college days must end as quickly as possible was to allow that stain to be bleached away by true adulthood, such was his belief in it. Little did he know the world he was about to step into was no place for cleansing.

He walked to the office where the school newspaper editors sat lounging in a conference room in the Student Union and handed it to them without saying more than three words before walking away, and to his surprise they published it. After deciding to submit it, his biggest challenge had been what pen name to use, because there was no way he would allow his real name to be attached to it. It would be bad enough if people didn't like it, and downright horrible if they did. It was a piece of crap, after all. He finally came up with a fitting pun for a name, Mike Ro-Amp. That didn't seem like a real enough fake name, so he took the hyphen out and signed it Mike Roamp. Maybe someone would like the pun at least, if they took the time to decipher it. They had much more of a chance of that than making sense of the poem itself. When he saw it in print in the hands of a guy he was passing in the quad and imagined it being read by hundreds of his peers, he was perplexed by his spirit soaring while his heart contracted against the chill of the biting winter wind as he walked to his haven past the glowing piles of snow.

16. The Scientist's Dilemma

Galesburg was not far away from Canton geographically, forty miles give or take, but in terms of the basketball landscape it was very distant. Thirty some thousand souls resided there, making it twice the size of Canton, and every year the high schools played each other in all sports, the larger town crushing the smaller with the certainty of the moon waning from full to half in a week's time. Benchwarmers on Galesburg's varsity would be stars if they wore Canton's uniforms, and Canton's stars would be lucky to make Galesburg's team. Both times they played earlier that year, Jimmy's senior year, the game was decided by the end of the third quarter, and the guys on the ends of both benches, which was where Jimmy resided, played most of the fourth quarter, and Jimmy had put on one of his best end of game performances against them in his last high school game. When the stat sheets were published you'd think he played starter's minutes, which wasn't saying all that much since four of Canton's starters averaged less than six points a game and blocking shots and making steals were easier against the scrubs.

So he'd seen most of the guys in action who were now on the court that summer, when a friend from his church took him to play a pickup game with the Galesburg varsity. That was not, as was so often the case, the reason the two of them were in Galesburg, days just happened to unfold that way in the circles in which Jimmy traveled. They were there to drop off some church related item at his friend's aunt's house, in the way in which teen aged boys were sent on errands, not knowing or caring what they were carrying, just happy to be given the keys to the car without true adult supervision. And in what was to them normal fashion, Cool Boy Stew, as he was known to Jimmy and Sonny, who had thusly named him, and not because he really thought he was all that cool, saw one of his hoopin' buddies walking down the street in his hoopin' gear and called out to him to find out where the game was. After the package was dropped off the rendezvous was made, and there stood Jimmy again, on a backyard concrete court wearing borrowed sneakers that did not fit because he hadn't brought any of his own, with a group of bigger, faster, stronger, guys who he had watched wipe the floor with the teammates his coaches thought should be playing instead of him, and he was in ecstasy. Another chance, randomly given, to prove his love.

Three Pointers

Scientists think of such simple things.
Thoughts of a drunk are much more complex
As they weave in and out of reality.
A genius is so simple minded
He can put his whole mind on one simple idea
And carry it to the limit.
You cannot let intelligence go to your head or
Ego can control the direction
In which logic will conquer goals,
But intelligence resides inside your head. Complicating things.
While scientists think of simple things.

Do you ever wonder why a baby cries when its born?
The sexual revolution was founded by loneliness.
People had to reach out past the modern society
Which tends to put each in his own corner.
A baby can't be lonely in the womb.

If I could only share your thoughts,
If I could only feel your pain,
We would be in harmony.
But then we would not need voices.
The sensation of your warm skin would never thrill me,
The heat which smells in my nostrils as joy.
And could we survive, then, apart?
Yes, we could, if only we but cry.

The scientist rubbed the back of his neck in relaxation.
A lesson can be learned from every and each page.

Cool Boy Stew was a preacher's kid, and his father preached at Jimmy's church. He was taller than Jimmy and thicker, even though he was still slim, and was as deeply immersed in his desires for the same lover as Jimmy was, so they had played often over the last couple of years, mostly one on one or in vicious games of Fight with Sonny forming a trio. He had always, or more accurately eight times out of ten, won these contests, when grabbing and pushing were not fouls and there was no one to pass to. It became even more necessary to his ego to dominate after Jimmy had made the Canton varsity in his senior year, a feat CBS could not replicate at his high school in Galesburg. It was Stew who demanded Jimmy put on the too wide shoes with a hole in the top of the right canvas upper. He wanted to prove to Jimmy the guys he looked up to, that he had bragged to Jimmy and Sonny about all the time, were well above Jimmy's talent level. Wearing the right shoes would not make a difference, he should understand, he'd get schooled wearing the latest Adidas, so he should just get out there and take the lesson.

It turned out to be more typical than even Jimmy imagined. Lazy passes were stolen, clever bounces led to text book assists, and in the moment when the power of the relationship changed forever, Jimmy stripped the ball from CBS, who was playing on the other team, at half court, in front of all his boys. CBS did something he knew from so many pickup games he should never do, and that was he should never dribble the ball in front of Jimmy more than once. The second bounce was Jimmy's, every time. Everyone, including Stew, laughed as they saw the rip coming and Jimmy dribbling down the court for the layup.

But that wasn't the play that sealed the deal for the rest of the players. They didn't think CBS was that much of a player, maybe he could have replaced some other guy who sat the bench, but no more, so ripping him at mid-court wasn't that great a feat in their minds. That memory happened on another play when Jimmy was out front in transition, and the outlet pass came late, and so high above his head he had to make an acrobatic leap along the baseline to snare it, landing with his left foot barely inside the line and his legs spread wide into the court. His opponents had recovered while he soared for the catch and when he came down had him trapped, with their big man - six five and menacing - standing with his legs spread wider than Jimmy's, staring down between him and the basket, and a second man sealing the trap along Jimmy's right side.

The big man wasn't just anyone to Stew and the rest of the crew. He was the playground legend of Galesburg, Guy Pierce, a guy who, according to Stew, anyway, could dunk with both hands, either hand, reversing, blind folded, any way he could dream up. He was slender at six five, and not growing any taller, so he was not the kind of guy who was headed for a major college career or professional riches, but at this stage of his life none of the guys who would eventually outgrow him had done so yet. He could jump higher than anyone, and moved with the kind of grace that made it seem like he was blocking your shot in slow motion. Jimmy had watched it a few times before, but never from this perspective. He was thinking of one thing, how to get the ball out of his hands and escape unharmed.

But then, one of Jimmy's teammates, a big white guy he had seen starting for Galesburg the year before, who had thrown him the ball late and put him in this bad spot in the first place, cried out, "Sorry man, throw it back!!"

Another teammate said, "Yeah, you got the pass!!" waving his arms to solicit being the target.

And that to Jimmy was an insult. What, they assumed he couldn't score from here? While being insulted Jimmy had already started his motion to throw it back out, stepping toward his outlet with his right leg and angling his arms to make the throw around the waving hands surrounding him, but the words froze his arms in mid-stroke. Both defenders leaned to block the pass they foresaw leaving Jimmy's hands, and when Jimmy saw they had committed themselves to making a steal, not blocking a shot, he knew he had them. He stretched out his arms to bait them to stretch further, then he stepped toward the baseline with his right leg and exploded quickly off both feet. Guy Pierce was quick for a big man, but he had to twist his body against his own momentum to lunge in the opposite direction as it was now clear where the ball was going, and that was straight to the basket. The lefty layup from the right side of the rim was admired by all, especially Guy as he swatted at it in vain, and the other defender who could not gather himself quickly enough to leap to block it.

"Damn, you got the shot!!!" said his amazed cohort.

Why this memory floated into his head during his frenzied drive to Canton that day made little sense to Jimmy. He had been studying, writing down equations and formulas like he always seemed to be doing when he wasn't doing something else, when the phone rang, and his mother's frantic voice was heard over the ether.

"Your Dad is in the hospital!! He had an accident mowing the lawn!!" was shouted out of the receiver.

"I'm on my way," was Jimmy's equally emotional response.

"No, don't come," said his mother, "He'll be OK."

"OK, Mom," said Jimmy. "See you in less than an hour."

And it turned out he was OK, since he didn't really need all ten of his fingers anymore anyway. Eight would have to be enough from then on. The time saved cutting the missing nails would be balanced by gloves never fitting on one hand. He had retired and was only working part time by this point, so his income was not severely damaged, but his pride and place in the family hierarchy were never the same. The era of parental invincibility was over. It was time for his son to take the reins of his own life, and put down his toys and take up his work tools. Watching his father rub the stubs that once were his right middle and ring fingers as he meekly explained what had transpired was all the visual proof Jimmy needed. His father had never looked so old and helpless, so resigned to his dwindling mortality. It was now time for Jimmy to become the pillar others would use to anchor themselves against the cold blasts of the future. He had to start pouring his own foundation, and no frivolous activities could take priority over this sacred task. The beloved, used to being the center of the universe, never understand when maturity smothers childhood and retaliate with extreme cruelty when adult concerns take precedence over their every whim in the hearts of their lovers, and Jimmy would not escape the wrath that follows the choice he had to make. That was still a long distance away, but it was no longer over the horizon, it was in plain sight.

17. War Bride

She was a check in the minus column,
Another reason to be a winner.
He loved her 'cause she had nothing to give
And asked for nothing in return.

He was young enough to realize
What he did was wrong.
He was old enough to live each day
As if it was his last,
'Cause it could be.

When they met over passion's necessity
She gave him all he was told to need.
Knowing he deserved none of it,
He spread out his heart like a doormat.

He cried when he realized he'd been lied to.
Life might be too short to rejoice in the spoils.
She had not had a break in her life,
But she refused to break his heart.

She gave birth to a crusader
Who did battle with the infidel of his conscience.
His young heart was too wealthy
To accommodate his wizened soul.

Three Pointers

He told her of watching his third best friend bleed,
Of finding a stranger's lonely arm.
He wanted to fill the void in her life
His own squeezing finger may have created.

When he told those he fought for of his new love,
They wrote back singing the blues.
Asking him to question the validity of his emotions;
Wasn't he too quick with his song?

But he knew life was an instant,
A snapshot that may not develop.
He was a check in the minus column,
A good reason for not playing the game.

And he loved her 'cause he had taken what she had,
She knew not to turn down a free ride.
You don't learn a thing from winning,
Losers go to school.

After winning the TKE game the Goodfellas were in the finals of the Holiday Tournament. In what was a surprise to Jimmy, but not to Hal and Grassman, at least, the championship game was not to be played in Haussler Hall in front of a few scores of people, it was to be held in the Fieldhouse, on the varsity's home floor, and it would take place as the first game of a double bill, the varsity playing in the second. That meant the game would start with only a couple of dozen in attendance, but by the start of the second half the stands would be filling, and by the end of the game thousands of Braves fans, and basketball fans in general, would be watching.

Jimmy couldn't remember the first time he was in this gym, maybe for a Christmas pageant when he was very small, maybe for a game while he was a school boy, and he had been sitting in the stands and watching others play ball many times since becoming a student at Bradley. He never thought he'd be standing on the court himself, in a layup line waiting for his turn to trot though the lane and catch the pass. From the moment Jimmy stepped onto it he was reminded of the high school gymnasium he played in for years before leaving for college. The building itself was a larger version of his former gym, with the barrel vaulted ceiling and lights twinkling from the rafters, the same depth of field behind the glass backboards, the same type of wooden floor, except in the Fieldhouse it was polished like glass and seemed free of dead spots, and was elevated three or four feet above the team benches and the first rows of seats. Everything was scaled up, including the court itself, the longest and widest on which Jimmy had ever played, and the stands rose into the darkness far higher than his high school's, but it still felt like a place he had dribbled and shot in before. The only thing which felt different was the scoreboard hanging above the middle of the court, well beyond the budget of a small-town school, which had the clock, score, and players' numbers lit up on each of the four sides. It seemed to radiate heat, such was the energy surging through him, and he was unable to keep from bouncing from foot to foot to imaginary music as he waited his turn. A huge smile would not leave his face. This stage was not intimidating him, and Jimmy made sure to let his boys know it. It was the time to shine, not hide.

The Kings were reformulated and Shack-less, but they were the heavy favorites for good reason. They still had Eddie and Tray to lead the way, and they picked up two big burly white guys, six-five and six-six, who only came out of the weight room to play ball a couple of times a week, the kind of guys who loved to mix it up under the boards and punish anyone who ventured down the lane with the ball or without, but didn't need to score much to be happy. Throughout the first half the Kings proved they were a little better at everything - shooting, passing, rebounding and defending - than the Goodfellas, and led by five by the time the horn sounded for intermission.

When the teams returned to the court after halftime the best evidence of the increase in the crowd was the murmur from the stands. What had been individual voices echoing around the arena was now a hushed roar. The bright lights shining down on the court made the people in the darkness of the stands invisible to the players, but the sound was steadily increasing, and it was impossible for the players to not hear it. There were chuckles and groans throughout the building when the Kings began the half with two straight baskets, stretching the lead to nine before a minute had elapsed. What might have been an interesting preliminary was turning into an unwatchable farce. The look on Hal's face and his body language said he agreed when he reached down slowly to pick up the ball as it bounced on the base line after falling through the net.

At the exact moment Jimmy was staring at Hal, his cousin Aileen came into view, walking below the baseline to her courtside seat. She had graduated from high school sports stars to college stars, and was dating one of the Bradley starters. When Jimmy saw her, he felt like losing this game would bring shame to his entire family, like letting the kid in her back yard show him up would have done, and he couldn't tolerate the look of defeat he saw in his teammates' eyes.

He shouted at Hal and Tyrone, who stood alongside Hal with both hands on his hips, loud enough for the entire Fieldhouse to hear him, "We, the three of us, right here, are going to bring this team back!!! We are NOT going to lose this game!! You hear me???"

He could tell he had shocked his mates. They were not in the mood to be called out like this. To be told they had to try harder would be acceptable, but to be told they were going to win? That took boldness. They had to be bold to take on this challenge.

"You hear me?????" screamed Jimmy to the startled onlookers. Aileen stopped in her tracks, transfixed by her relative, the one she remembered as being so weak and sickly, standing there like a tower of testosterone, starkly demanding others to follow him into the lion's den.

"Yeah," said Tyrone, not too convincingly as Hal inbounded the ball.

"Right now!!!" Jimmy called out again as he began to dribble up court.

Tray was waiting for him, at the top of the key, with a look of derision on his face. Everyone had heard what Jimmy had said. Now was the time to shove those words back down his throat. Jimmy stared hard at him, then stuck his left foot into the wood and pushed off, blasting past Tray by only a quarter step, his defender trailing as he tried to match the explosive move. Jimmy couldn't shake Tray and didn't want to, he wanted to do what came next, and that was for Tray, and Eddie, and both the brutes they had down low to converge, waiting for some fancy move or pass, and to plow right into them. This was about proving intent. To win this game the Goodfellas had to go through the Campus Kings, not around them. The time to start was right now.

The whistle blew, and Tray was charged with the foul. He was reaching while Jimmy was plowing, an attempt that ended with bodies crashing and the ball floating out of bounds after hitting the side of the backboard. As he walked to the line he knew he had to keep up the pressure.

"Tray can't guard me, and everyone here knows it," Jimmy said loud enough for all standing along the lines to hear as he stood waiting for the ball. He was so hyped up he couldn't focus on his routine, and he missed the first free throw.

Tray trotted over to him and cooed softly, "You can't handle the pressure, can you?" as the referee retrieved the errant shot and Jimmy waited for his second. That was just what Jimmy needed.

Smiling, he took the ball and repeated the same sequence he had practiced for more than a decade, but as he took the three bounces he normally did, he turned once again to the players standing in their places along the lane and repeated, "Tray cannot guard me." And to his mates, "Just give me the ball." And the second shot dropped through the net with all the angry purpose he could spin into it.

The game turned from that point. Now it was the Goodfellas who rebounded a bit harder, who defended a bit stingier, who made the tougher shots. It was still hand to hand fighting, fouls more frequent than field goals, but as the minutes trudged on so did the Goodfellas; slowly, inexorably, boring through the mountain with complete disdain for climbing it. Both sides were expending tremendous amounts of energy surging ahead and stemming the tide, and by the time the clock read less than one minute to play the Kings had the ball but not enough strength to hold it or score it and they turned it over to the Goodfellas with thirty seconds left and one more point to score to make the comeback complete.

During the time out Large Louis mapped out a play, but as the huddle broke Jimmy turned to Tyrone and said, "Here's what we're gonna do. I'm gonna dribble the ball right down their throats, and then I'm gonna pass you the ball, and then you're gonna score and we're gonna win this thing. You hear me????"

And so it went, exactly as Jimmy scripted it. He slowly brought the ball up court, faked left and went right and Tray tried to cut him off but couldn't, and Jimmy thought for an instant of taking it all the way but couldn't, as his legs had been betraying him for the last few minutes and had nothing left in them to make the needed push. Instead he lofted a pass to Tyrone who was not open unless he could out jump everyone which he did, and then he went strong against Eddie and put up a sweet bank shot that looked to the crowd as if it was surely going to fall but it didn't, instead bouncing high before caroming off the rim a second time. As it rose Jimmy's heart sank, another near miss leading to a close loss just a rebound away, but Tyrone was having none of that. He leapt again above the crowd of Kings and snatched the rebound, this time going up so strong and true the ball had no choice but to drop through the net. Goodfellas up by one.

Jimmy had no illusions of this game being over, even though he raised his hands in victory as the shot fell through. He did what the point guard was supposed to do. Instead of watching the last 10 seconds run down while dancing in circles, as most of his teammates were doing, he bolted to half court to watch for a long pass. Tray took the ball out of bounds and spotted Eddie running down the side line, the only hope for a last second shot, and heaved it, his only choice. Jimmy was in perfect position to defend it, but his legs had no spring to leap in front of the oncoming train to steal the pass. Instead he set his feet and waited, knowing Eddie would have to make a sudden move to avoid charging into him after catching it himself. Eddie made a beautiful leaping grab, making a half turn in the air to snag it, and took a dribble straight ahead with his head down, eyes staring at the floor - there was no time to look for anyone anyway - and plowed into Jimmy, standing in perfect position, right out of the textbook for taking a charge, his feet spread but not moving, and he took the contact full into his chest, not falling before taking the blow as so many do. Eddie could only survive the collision by stumbling to his right, a fantastic spin move - if that had been his intention instead of being what the law of action and reaction forced him to do - and made two staggering dribbles across the court toward a waiting Tyrone, who had also kept his head and sprinted down the court after making the shot. Eddie threw up a prayer as the buzzer sounded, and Tyrone stood still and watched him launch it instead of jumping for the block. The ball floated for what seemed like minutes, so high it might have touched the scoreboard if it had been released a little closer to half court, before it tipped the top of the backboard and fell straight down like an arrow from the quill of Cupid's evil twin and through the net.

Jimmy's vantage was from his back, where he remained sprawled after being run over, and he knew it was going to fall from the instant it left Eddie's hands. He didn't deserve it yet. He hadn't suffered enough. If he had been in better shape they would have caught up quicker and the last second shot wouldn't have mattered. If he had been the leader in the first half he was in the second, the game might not have even been close. He rolled over, slammed his fists into the floor so loudly the entire celebration, the hugging mob of Kings at center court and all those watching from their seats or walking down the aisles with their popcorn, turned to look at the defeated man still on his knees near half court.

It didn't help when Tyrone admitted later, "I could have blocked that shot, but I was lookin' over at the ref, waitin' for him to blow his whistle. I mean, he ran you over, man."

It also didn't help when he heard the same thing again and again and again until the semester ended, and he retreated to his ten lap per mile track at the Y in Canton.

Analog computer lab was no fun, made much worse by the knowledge of it being a complete waste of time. Within ten years, maybe five, no one would be using analog computers anymore. Despite all the heavyweights of technology still relying on them in 1981, analog electronics were being superseded by solid state, all digital circuits which replaced what an analog circuit did with current and voltage with discrete ones and zeros. Analog was a smooth flow of data, real time devices charging and discharging at a steady parabolic rate, while digital was packets of infinitesimally small yes's and no's, counted until a verdict was given by something called a processor. The future was in the metallurgy of silicon and germanium that would allow smaller and smaller transistors - not in the bulky inductors and capacitors and resistors, the transistor op amps with 5 legs reaching down to the connection board at which Jimmy was staring.

He had to diagram, then execute, a circuit which would solve a differential equation he had been assigned and use the computer to watch the mathematics play out on an oscilloscope, which he could then graph as the proof of his successful completion of the task. As seniors, they were given assignments and deadlines and were on their own to find time to get them done, and had the pass to enter the lab any time a class wasn't in session, which meant with fifty students and only one analog computer, Jimmy was sitting on a stool at eleven thirty at night, gazing at the potentiometers and lights and switches of the soon to be obsolete beast he was assigned to tame. After driving back from Canton he had marched straight to the lab, too engaged in his thoughts of the future to sleep, and too close to his deadline to spend the night with other pursuits. It was almost three before he had untangled his mind from its mysteries and, like an ancient stargazer descending from his perch after the clear night sky gave way to dark clouds, walked silently across the quad sharing his moist breaths with the night air.

18. Modern Windows

Someone was pounding on Jimmy's dorm room door, and when he opened it, a happy, smiling face he never expected to see was staring at him. He knew who it was, a guy he met at the gym named Will Masters, but why he was standing in his doorway made no sense. It kind of made more sense when he looked down and saw a basketball in his hands, but not really, as the gym was not open for ballers this early in the day.

"Come on, man," said Will after the required "wassup's", "Let's go over to this court I know and play some ball."

Jimmy looked at Will and immediately knew there was more to this story than met the eye. It was a setup of some kind. He had experienced it so many times he could smell it pouring out of Will's pores. He did a quick summation. Will was a track star in high school, Jimmy had been told but didn't know if he believed he had won first place in the hurdles in the state meet a couple of years before. He was well known and very popular among the varsity basketball and baseball stars, so he must have done something, and he was considered a prize to the ladies, or so he considered himself. Jimmy had embarrassed Will a few times the year before on the basketball court, once in front of several of the cutest girls in the school, and Will had to grin and bear it at the time. They had always been cordial toward each other. Will was quick to smile and make friends, but an athlete's pride runs deeper than friendship, especially a superficial one. This must be about some sort of payback.

To make sure, Jimmy asked, "Who else is playin?"

"Just me and you, man," said Will.

So he couldn't say no. Plus it was the start of a new fall semester, and what better way to ease into the routine of studying than a hoop break? After putting on his gear he followed Will down the stairs and straight down Elmwood until they turned toward the entrance of University Hall, the dorm housing ninety percent of the freshman girls, plus a few upperclasswomen sprinkled in for supposedly increased sanity. On the back side of the building, facing the windows of half of the rooms, was a small outdoor half court, with a concrete floor and an unstable wooden backboard which twisted slightly but noticeably when the ball was thrown against it.

Now it was clear. Will was after his revenge, and he wanted as many girls to witness it as possible. He couldn't have made it easier for them. He had probably bragged about the lesson he was about to give to a few of them before disturbing Jimmy from his perusal of his Electrical Circuit Theory book. That thought made Jimmy smile, as Will had inadvertently conceded Jimmy had a high hoops quotient or the girls would not be impressed by Will's beating him.

As they warmed up, Jimmy watched Will and realized he had made a miscalculation. Will was previously embarrassed by Jimmy, and it was about to happen again, because he had a bad habit he hadn't been practicing to correct over the summer. He dribbled the ball too high, he put it in front of his body too often, and worst of all he liked to "Pearl," which was a pretty move, but unless he was as quick as Earl "the Pearl" Monroe, which he wasn't, would result in a steal when Jimmy was guarding him, by slipping behind him and stripping the ball at the top of the dribble. Jimmy's friend Sonny loved to "Pearl" as well, and over the many hours of playing against him Jimmy had developed the strip move.

So that was how the game went. Will couldn't dribble the ball without pushing off or Jimmy would tip it away, and when he did get off a shot Jimmy would more than likely alter it. Jimmy began by shooting mostly jump shots, working on his accuracy, plus not in much danger of losing the game since Will couldn't score. As the game wore on, the years he spent playing forward against bigger guys made it easy for the skinnier but longer armed Jimmy to back Will down and make shots around the block to seal the deal. Before it was over an unseen voice, a guy both Jimmy and Will knew, was providing play-by-play for the unseen onlookers by shouting out of a window. He was cheering Jimmy on more than anything, laughing at the blocked shots and steals, trying to make Will look as foolish in front of his supposed admirers as he could. There were all types of competitions going on, and since Jimmy was not considered that kind of player, building him up was not seen as a threat. When the game ended Will slapped Jimmy on the back and laughed as he conceded defeat.

"Let me know when you want a rematch," called out Jimmy as he trotted back toward his dorm and Will turned to enter the girls'. He never did.

The playoffs began in April, with the Open and Frat Divisions having their championships before spring break and the All-University Championship Tournament, pitting the two finalists from each division in a four-team bracket, occurring immediately after. The Goodfellas cruised through the Open Division, reaching the final without having to endure a single nervous moment, and were heavily favored against their surprise opponents, the squad Eddie Morris played on, The Fog.

The player/coach of the Fog, a guy so loud-mouthed while exclaiming his coaching acumen it was assumed he was from Indiana, but he wasn't, had brashly predicted a victory in the title game, and said he had the perfect strategy to pull it off. The Fog, in addition to Eddie, had his little brother Evan, who Jimmy could thank for the dislocated pinky on his right hand, courtesy of Evan jamming a loose ball into it during a pick-up game earlier that year, a finger that would never again be straight for the rest of Jimmy's life. Two more big guys and two short little guards who could light it up on rare occasions rounded out the squad.

The day of the final was one of the rarest of rare occasions, when both the Fog guards were incendiary from the opening horn until the final whistle ended the tussle. Neither before this game, nor after this game, did the Fog hit this many outside bombs, which was just about the only way they could score. Inside they were outmatched, so they packed everyone tightly in a zone and depended on their guards to win the resultant jump shooting contest. Early in the second half Jimmy, who was getting run around screen after screen when he wasn't getting picked trying to chase the shorter sharpshooter he was guarding, stepped awkwardly and twisted his right knee, going down hard and writhing on the floor in agony. Ankles he had twisted plenty of times, and since he did not weigh much they were never severe, but a knee was something different. Maybe once, when playing football in the snow on the playground he had felt this kind of pain, but that was from a direct hit inside the knee, not from a twist like this. After a full minute he adjusted to the pain still flowing from the contorted ligaments in his leg and stood, and with a grit of his teeth walked to the bench without a limp. If he limped, Grassman, who had been kneeling next to him before he rose, would never let him back in the game.

He didn't anyway. The fall he had taken looked much worse to the others than it felt to Jimmy after he had sat and stretched it for a while, and when he tapped Grassman on the shoulder to be put back in it was to no avail. He sat and watched the rest of the half along with the other startled fans, as the Fog rained jumper after jumper into the net past the defenseless Goodfellas until the last minute of the game. To add a sweet little cherry on the top of their title Eddie got the ball on a fast break, one on one against Tyrone, and made him look foolish with a smooth reverse layup. The horn sounded, the game ended, and the Fog were Open Division champions.

Being forced to watch them go down in defeat made Jimmy livid and he let his teammates know it. The response he received was shocking, but in the face of what had just happened, not surprising.

Hal looked at him and asked with derision, "If you couldn't stop him before you twisted your knee, how'd you think you were gonna do it after?"

"The rest of you guys couldn't stop him either," said Jimmy incredulously. "He's never been that hot in his life!"

After dancing around with his teammates, Eddie sat in the stands cooling down next to Jimmy like they were not opponents a few minutes before. Jimmy turned to him and said, "You ready?"

Eddie had a look of surprise, but not in shock as he responded, "If you are."

"If you can drive, I am."

And with that the friends put on their sweats and walked to Jimmy's car, which he had parked outside the gym to save some steps, and were on the road to Canton, for Jimmy's next game of the night.

Regardless of the outcome of the game - both Jimmy and Eddie had assumed the Goodfellas would win the title game, since they had beaten the Fog rather handily during the regular season – the pair had planned to go to Canton together, and the fact the Fog had won wasn't going to change that. However, what about the twisted knee? In Jimmy's mind not playing would be far worse than playing, as the knee would swell more, plus at twenty-two his body's powers of recovery were at their peak and injuries had short memories, and sure enough after an hour his knee was beginning to forget it was ever twisted. Running on it would do nothing but hasten it entering its firm future and turning away from its feeble past.

When the 365er's ran through their warm ups, there was no sign of a limp and only a remnant of the pain, and the sharp edges of the earlier loss were smoothed by a hard-fought victory with his high school crew. After closing his eyes at midnight he dreamed of the next dawn, glowing with fresh, new promise, and closed his mind to the bitter, stale air of the past.

I.
Modern windows
Opening into technology
Skyscraper sandpaper
To brush against the sky
To clean the filth of society.

Middle of the road patriot
The chief protector of
The right to conform to be free
Looking through the portal
With the awe of a child.

II.
Dawn doesn't break, it overwhelms
Running headlong towards the night
Never to quite reach.
A motion of perpetual change.

Wonder how you smile tonight
Since sadness is the lone emotion I can muster.
What is it you know that makes you so sure
Or what is it I shouldn't have learned?

You protect my sanity
And cobwebs of childishness are swept away,
But don't let me dive into the deep end
Of a place I've no right to be.

Gallantry is dead, and love cheapened to
Make it easier to be soft.

But you be soft for me…

19. It is Immortal

The Goodfellas held a team meeting after the Fog game. Everyone was furious about losing and the team was close to fracturing. The main topic of discussion was who should be starting in the All-U Tournament. The debate was based on the fact the inside guys felt the guards had played terrible defense and that had led to their defeat, and something had to change. Accusations and incriminations abounded, and after all had spit their personal venom into the room, the ones to be included in the starting five were put to a vote. The starters voted in were Hal, Tyrone, Darrell, Mike Marsh and Paul Carpenter. When the votes were tallied, and it became obvious to everyone Jimmy wasn't picked, they started to backtrack.

Tyrone started it. "Wait, Jimmy didn't get picked?"

Jimmy was quick to respond, as he had never been quite this angry in his life. "You didn't vote for me, did you? In fact, I only got one vote, and I voted for myself."

Hal explained, "I voted for who was playing the best defense."

Jimmy stared at Hal, then looked over at Paul, who looked down at the floor, knowing he couldn't play any defense if his curly locks depended on it.

Instead of denigrating the freshman, Jimmy changed the subject. "Who is going to play the point? If it's not me, it's gotta be Jerry. No one else can get the ball up court!"

His anger was turning to disgust. Here he was, in his last semester, on a team that had made it to the All-U Tournament, and they were not going to let him start?

"Well," said Grassman, realizing he had to take back control of the team, "No matter who got voted in, if you don't show up to practice the day we get back from break, you're not starting. In fact, the first five guys there will start."

With that the group broke up and went their separate ways silently before anyone could say anything else stupid enough to start another row before spring break. Not one team member saw another for the next week.

Three Pointers

Used to see you all the time,
Wishing I could make you mine.
'Cross the crowded noisy room,
I would sit there, lonely as a tomb.
You'd be busy with your crowd,
Dancing eyes so soft and proud.
All the time erasing the fact I was there,
I knew you knew – I caught your stare.
In touch with feelings of you on my mind,
Injured by living in a world so unkind,
As to make you and I blasphemous, heresy, sin -
To force us to choices that humble most men.
The lukewarm flow of the status quo
Will not let our inhibitions go,
And love that should be nourished and fed
Lies trampled in the dust, left for dead –
But it is immortal.

When Canton played Galesburg in the regionals in 1977, the Little Giants were more than twenty points down mid-way through the fourth quarter and Coach Bucky cleared the bench, letting Jimmy loose to do whatever he wanted on the court in his last game before graduating from high school. Even earlier in the season, when in the coach's mind at least he might have earned more minutes by sticking with the offense and not always creating chaos, he couldn't follow the prescribed pattern of the Canton scheme, especially when he had seen that scheme put the team down by 24 points like he had seen so many times before that season. Whenever he was allowed on the court he would show the coach how the team should be playing, the scrappy style a bunch of undersized hustlers needed to play to have any success against bigger, stronger teams, but that had only earned him a spot further down the bench to watch slaughter after slaughter. But this last time it did not matter.

When he entered the game Jimmy was assigned to guard a kid with one of the biggest Afros Jimmy had ever seen, which was saying something because in 1977 there were many, many huge balls of hair on the heads of many, many, ballers. After admiring what had to take hours to keep picked out, Jimmy looked under the hair and realized the kid wasn't all that tall. He couldn't believe it when the kid caught a pass, wing extended, and jumped up for a shot like Jimmy wasn't standing right in front of him. He couldn't believe even more when the kid was surprised when Jimmy swatted the ball straight up into the air after it left his hand. They both waited, jostling for position as the ball floated up, then down between them and they jumped in unison for it. Instead of grabbing at it like his opponent Jimmy spotted Watay sprinting up the court, anticipating what was coming, and swatted at the ball again, this time in the direction of his teammate. It spun away from the fingers of his opponent and into the outstretched arms of his mate, who then raced down court for an easy lay in. In the next five and a half minutes Jimmy darted around the floor like a bee in a lush garden from rebound, to tip in, to open jumper, to steal, and when the buzzer sounded to bring down the lights of his varsity life he had eight points, two rebounds, one steal, one block, and an assist, and you'd have thought he played most of the game if you only looked at the box score.

Jimmy and Jerry were the first ones to practice. Jimmy picked Jerry up because he had an idea, and that idea was for Jerry to start at point guard and for Jimmy to revert to off-guard. If another team was going to shoot the lights out against them, they needed as much offensive fire power as possible, and Jimmy was the best one to provide it. And since their first game was against Delta Nu, the Frat League champs, they would need to score some points for sure. So Jimmy drove his car and used some of the last precious drops in his gas tank to pick Jerry up and make sure he was at the gym early. When Hal and Tyrone and Darrell showed up next, and tallied the starting five, they were relieved and concerned at the same time.

Jerry was by far the most talented and best suited point guard on their team, but he was prone to mental lapses, and the usual result of those lapses was turnovers. Once he made one he would begin to press, and one multiplied into a bunch, and the team would turn on him and the coach would have to sit him down. But on those occasions when he kept his head he was the perfect bulldog at the top of the key, quick enough to defend the quickest opponent and skilled enough to drive the lane and dish or score. The determining factor was always above his shoulders, not below.

So Jimmy knew by thrusting Jerry into the starting lineup he was volunteering to babysit his psyche until the next game and through the next game, and he let the skeptics in front of him know he knew what was necessary.

"I'm gonna play off-guard for the tourney," he announced before they could voice their concerns, "and Jerry's gonna run the point. I'll take full responsibility for getting him ready."

He could tell they were not convinced, but Jimmy was not to be deterred.

"Look guys, this is my last chance. I'm the only senior on this team. I told you guys from the moment I joined you last year that I thought we could win the All-U's, and here it is right in front of us. I don't care about all the times before when we lost games we should have won. I don't care about the Holiday freakin' Tournament when we got robbed. I told you then and I'm telling you now, all I care about is winnin' the freakin' All-U's!! Period."

He paused now, and the look he gave each man listening to his speech let them know they owed him this, and more importantly they could trust him with the outcome. He wasn't waiting until it was too late this time.

"And we're gonna win it. Guaranteed. I'll make sure of it," he concluded, grabbing Jerry around the neck like the little brother he had adopted for the next few days.

They started and ended the practice with wind sprints, something unheard of for intramural teams, with Jimmy insisting and then leading the way. Forward full court, backward full court, line drills, slides, the whole lot. Never had the churning and burning in their guts brought such joy.

20. Don't Ever Give Up on Love

Delta Nu set the new record as the biggest front line in the history of Bradley intramurals. Once their bitterest rivals, the TKE house, won the All-U's the year before, the Deltas had gone to great lengths to find the tallest pledges they could and recruited a pair of bulky six-six guys and a six-seven bean pole to tower over all their adversaries. They hadn't lost a game since losing to the Campus Kings in the Holiday Tournament the semester before and rumor had it the best player in the Frat League had been added since then as one of their guards. They crushed the TKE's in the Frat semifinals, and that victory was so complete the final game, an even bigger blowout, was an anti-climax. The Deltas trotted onto the Fieldhouse court with their heads anointed and the prize preordained. The Goodfellas had beaten the TKE's the last semester as well, but it had been a difficult struggle, and this was a bigger stage, so all the Deltas had to do was play their normal steady game and it would end in victory, as their opponent would find a way to capitulate as they always did. Then they would have an even easier time in the championship game against the Fog.

By the time Jimmy pulled into the Fieldhouse parking lot he had thoroughly convinced Jerry he would star at the point in the game and lead the Goodfellas to the championship. Jimmy kept whispering this mantra into his ear during warmups to make sure no doubt could creep in. They would not play the slow down game Grassman had been preaching, when it was two on two and Jimmy and Jerry were out in front against the Delta Nu guards they were going to break them down hard. No slowing down. Straight to the hole. Take no prisoners.

The opening tip would tell the tale in short order. The ball was tipped ahead by Darrell to Jerry, who followed his orders when he saw Jimmy speeding up court and led him with a sharp long pass that was high and hard. Jimmy slowed as the pass left Jerry's hands, and what could have been a smooth leap to an easy layup became a strained lunge along the base line to catch what was sure to be the first turnover. Jimmy couldn't let that happen. Somehow, he elongated his body far enough to allow his fingertips to stick to the pebbles and remain inbounds as he landed.

"My bad!!" shouted Jerry, his mind already disbelieving the glory it had been filled with seconds before.

Jimmy's momentum was carrying him out of bounds giving him no choice but to square up his elbow as best as possible and let fly, knowing by instinct when and how to release the ball with the proper wrist flip and arm extension, something learned from being pushed off the court so many times before on the playground, with the hand of one of the Delta big men swatting down as he faded behind the backboard. Their hands clapped as the ball sailed upwards, its arc higher than the taller man could reach at the apex of his jump. Even though there was no other contact made, the sound of palms slapping brought the whistle to the referee's mouth. It blew as the ball fell from its lofty heights and slipped softly through the cords.

Two thoughts entered Jimmy's mind as he trotted to the free throw line to complete the three-point play and extend his team's lead to start the game. First was his point guard's confidence.

"Great pass, Jerry!!! My fault for not keepin' goin'!!! Do the same thing next time!!"

The second was knowing that shot was falling from the instant it left his hands and being filled with confidence they were all falling tonight. That first shot, the way he released it and the way it responded, was all a shooter needs to feel to be off on a tear. After drilling the free throw, not shooting it, he knew this night would not end as so many others. All the pleasures from the receipt of love poured into him as he ran down the court to play defense: the joy, the absence of gloom, the future a shining light full of promise, of fruitfulness, and the buoyantly impenetrable determination to fulfill all his young dreams of yesterday and tomorrow.

Three Pointers

Don't ever give up on love
If it hurts you know it's real
A myriad of change may happen in your lifetime
But givin' it up is living death.

Don't ever give up on hope
Or you cannot face the future
The search through the maze will seem pointless
You will sit and wait on the beast.

Don't ever give up on laughter
Your smile makes my dull days bright
Reminds me of unencumbered childhood
When my soul had full freedom of flight.

Don't ever give up on dreams
Or they cannot and will not come true
You have jumped overboard without reason
And will drown in a sea of regret.

And please, don't ever give up on me.

Terry Cummings was Chicago basketball legend. Born and raised on the South Side, he was a star at Carver High School, then went on to DePaul University, and along with Mark Aguirre, kept the school ranked in the top ten in the nation for a couple of years. He was drafted in the first round in 1982, and was named NBA rookie of the year in the spring of 1983. At the end of that season he was diagnosed with a heart problem and ordered to stop all athletic activities for the next few months until the medication prescribed took affect and corrected it. The summer day Jimmy met him was the day he returned from the doctor's office having been cleared to participate in "limited activities" on his path to a full recovery. After a quick stop at his mother's house to share the news and pick up a couple of partners, he drove his late model, bespoke Volvo to the local playground where it had all started for him and waited for the game in progress to end so he could play next.

And Jimmy just happened to have the rights to the next game and needed a couple of guys to round out his squad. It was a mini-reunion of the Goodfellas; Tyrone and Hal and Jimmy, on one of the local courts Hal had played on for years; even though Tyrone and Hal were playing skins and Jimmy had lost the last game with the shirts and was therefore waiting alongside the court when the Volvo arrived. Of course he agreed to let TC and his older brother Billy, who was the all-time legend of this court until his younger brother outgrew him by eight inches, run with him. Before the day was over, Jimmy, Tyrone and Hal all knew how the game they loved, and they thought loved them so much, was conducted at its highest level, and the love they had been given and thought was unconditional could at best be considered an infatuation by comparison.

175

It was obvious to Jimmy, anyway, that TC was playing at maybe 40% speed, but was still fast enough to trot down the court at the same pace as Jimmy's full sprint. And once when the ball was loose on the baseline and Jimmy reached it a split second before TC and grabbed it a fraction before he did, he had a revelation. Many times in this instance the bigger, stronger man had snatched the ball away from Jimmy's weaker grip, but never had that man been so strong he did not need to snatch it, he just lifted the ball with Jimmy still attached and leapt toward the rim to dunk it. If Jimmy hadn't been sharp enough to realize what was about to happen and let go of the ball, he would have been tossed against the backboard as part of the upcoming slam without TC even knowing he was there.

That dunk was not the epiphany for Tyrone. His came when he went up as strong as he knew how for a rebound, and found himself soaring far out of bounds, having bumped shoulders with TC on the way up. For Tyrone, who never bounced off anyone, or let anyone knock him off his spot legally, this could not have just happened.

"That was a foul!" he cried, but he looked at his teammates and saw no one backing him up, then looked at Jimmy, standing close by to hand him the ball after TC dunked it, and then Hal waiting for him to inbound him the ball, and asked, "Is he really that strong?"

Hal shrugged in Tyrone's direction, and Jimmy just stared at him. Tyrone took that as a "yes" and tossed Hal the ball and the game went on.

The "other guy" who came with TC and his brother played in the next game, which meant against Jimmy's squad, and he was also a beast. He played exactly like Jimmy played, except on a larger scale. His arms were longer, his legs were longer, and he was quicker than Jimmy, could jump higher, had more stamina, was bigger and stronger, there was no aspect of his game Jimmy could match. Even though Jimmy might have been a better shooter or even more technically sound in other areas, this guy's athleticism and sheer size trumped all that with ease. Jimmy was consumed with the thought, no, better yet, the reality, if he entered a contest with nine other beings this size he had little chance to come away unscathed, and maybe not even mobile. Love clearly had its limits, and despite what he had been told about the motion of the ocean, once size reached a critical order of magnitude it swamped all the ability, technical skill, and hours of practice a mere mortal like Jimmy could amass.

The Goodfellas never trailed in the game, keeping the margin comfortable throughout. The key became rebounding, and so long as they kept the bigger boys blocked out and off the offensive glass, there was no way for the Frat champs to come back. This was the game Darrell showed what he could do if he was ever angry enough to do it. After taking a couple of blows from the DU big boys early, he let his inner demons loose and the bodies falling to the sides had DU written on them, not Goodfellas, and he made his point clear to all with a thunderous rebound jam after a miss by Tyrone. He was playing with such a fury Jimmy had to ask Hal what had gotten into him.

"His girlfriend broke up with him. I've never seen him so pissed," explained Hal with a shrug and a smile.

"Can you make sure they don't get back together until after the final?" asked Jimmy.

It was that kind of game. Rugged action sprinkled with laughter and one-liners. During the second half DU scored twice in a row off offensive rebounds, so Jimmy started crashing the boards in support of his interior mates, flying in from his guard spot whenever a shot went up. He was greeted with elbows, forearms, shoulders, and never came closer than a tip to getting his hands on the ball.

After depositing him out of bounds for the third time, one of the big boys grabbed Jimmy around the waist to pick him up. He asked, "Are you gonna keep comin' down here and getting clobbered?" with a tone of warning and amusement.

"Yup!" replied a laughing Jimmy as he danced away. "See ya down here next time!"

It was understood. No quarter asked, no quarter given. Both men smiled as they looked in each other's eyes. When the game ended Jimmy led all participants in bumps, bruises and points, and the Goodfellas waltzed into the All-U finals with a convincing twelve-point win. Jerry made believers of everyone, finishing with only two turnovers in the game, and most importantly, never forgetting his duty to protect his own goal against streaking intruders, leaving not a single fast break uncontested.

21. One Day You Will Stop Dying

Once there was a paper in a stack,
It was so, so far from the top.
Even though more were added, sometimes, to the top,
It always rose higher.

A rocket ship springs from its nest on the ground,
Pushes out past the atmosphere.
But it will at some point reach the end of its thrust,
And float on the whim of the universe.

One day there will be no one born who dies before you,
One day you will stop dying.
One day you will loosen your hold on the nest,
Fly and fall, fall and fly,
Plotting your course with a true eye,
Until it flies out of your hands.

The Senior Lab course culminated in two separate and equally important presentations: the first being an oral dissertation on what the project was, the problem to be solved and the expected result, the mathematics behind it, the tools used, the method of construction, the documentation created, a synopsis of the results, ideas for improvements, and a summation in conclusion; or so it was outlined by Jimmy. The second being a demonstration, where the professors could put their hands on the hardware and pick apart the data, ask embarrassing questions, and frown with pleasure in the way only authoritative academics can.

Papichulo wore his best suit, solid brown with white stitching around the wide lapels and the large pockets, coordinated with a wide brown and yellow crocheted tie and matching yellow shirt, and to stay current with engineer fashion, white canvas gym shoes. He stood at the podium and delivered the speech they had written in his slurry accent with less confidence than usual as if the gravity of the situation was weighing down his vocal cords. He stumbled through the opening explanations of the major parts of the circuit they had built: the reference oscillator which generated the speed set point; the phase detector which compared two inputs, the actual speed of the motor and the set point signal; the low pass filter which eliminated any high frequency harmonics to send a pure error signal to the next circuit; the voltage controlled oscillator which transformed the error signal into a voltage output which was then fed into the final stage; the power driver, which in turn fed power to motor input terminals, speeding the motor up and down by increasing or decreasing the output to lock the motor's speed in phase with the reference signal. As Papichulo poured out the words Jimmy used the overhead projector to show the audience the block diagram of the entire system and then the individual circuitry which made up each block.

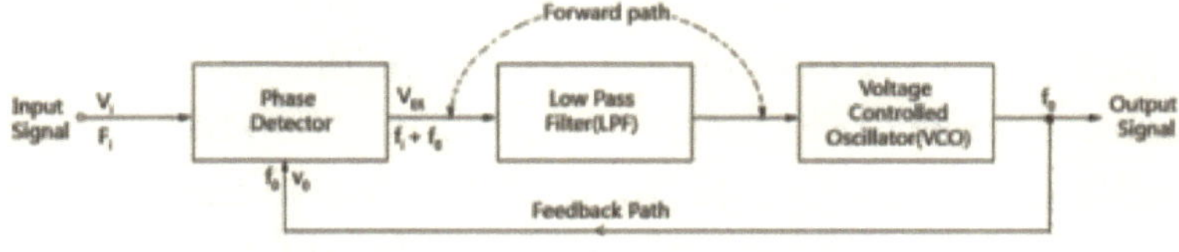

PLL Block Diagram

When it came to the explanation of the mathematical modeling of the system's response, the equations governing how their phase lock loop worked, Jimmy took Papichulo's place at the microphone and his partner manned the projector. They started with the equation governing the response of the entire loop, including the motor.

$$A_{OLC}(s) = \frac{K_\phi \times K_{LF}(s) \times G_{PD} \times N}{s^2 C_M \times K_V}$$

And then went on to the equation for the motor transfer function:

$$\frac{N \times \omega_M(s)}{i_M(s)} = \frac{N}{K_V} \times \frac{1}{s C_M}$$

Jimmy had to painstakingly explain, with constant interruptions for scholarly debate amongst the PhD's, the meaning of each element in the equations - such as the meaning and value of N, where the constant Kv's value was obtained, and on down the line - until the last professor's grunted question had been resolved.

Papichulo joined Jimmy for a joint description of the results. They were not a smashing success, but with a multitude of strip charts, oscilloscope graphs, and boisterous charm he made it through with only a couple of groans from the esteemed faculty. The system had worked, but the motor was torque limited and could not maintain the desired speed over the entire range of load. After scolding the soon to be professionals for not bringing this to their attention in time for them to help provide a remedy, the esteemed faculty had to concur with the soundness of the duo's design. In the end their classmates clapped and hollered to bring it to a close.

On his first full day on campus in his first year of college there was only one place for Jimmy to go to introduce himself to his new society. It wasn't the electronics lab, like some of his fellow nerds chose; or the freshman girls' dorm, like so many of the cool guys; it was Haussler Hall, the student athletic facility which held the indoor basketball courts. Nothing was more important to a large segment of the student population than to establish the hoops hierarchy for the coming year, and ranking high would make entry into the already established cliques possible. Not that Jimmy was into cliques, but he was into playing, not watching others play, and to do that took a reputation. Guys who looked like him had to prove it; they couldn't awe anyone with their physical presence alone. And on this day all the best players were there, from varsity guys not yet restricted by the first day of official practice, to the firmly established intramural stars, to the wanna-bes and hangers-on.

So he had to wait his turn with the wanna-bes and make it count when it came. Coming from a small town he was quite intimidated by what he had seen in the games played before his chance, and in his mind the level of play in Chicago and its environs, where most of the students hailed, especially the best players, was far beyond what he had ever encountered, and he might be overmatched. When he finally got into a game, with some of the varsity ballers along with some of the best on The Yard still hustling up and down the court with him, he stayed out of harm's way along the left baseline, and when the first pass came his way he shot it because he was too afraid of dribbling or passing, and the shot fell through the net with a practiced perfection. It was the baseline jumper proving to be his salvation again, and he proceeded to show those assembled he was a machine from that spot. When his opponents drove him off it after convincing themselves this was no fluke, he started draining shots from the wing. That first shot was all he needed to know it was one of those days shooters live for, when the rim draws the ball inside it like a magnet and all he had to do was let it go. Days like this were to be cherished and exploited, orchestrated to make others remember who he was the next time he stepped into the gym. By the time he unlaced his sneakers and sat in the bleachers watching those not worthy of running with the big dogs play out the last minutes of open gym, Jimmy had firmly moved out of the wanna-be column and into the up-and-comers.

22. At the Beginning

Dan Martin was the boss, no doubt about it, and he was on the rise. He carried himself with an imperial air, and he advertised his greatness equally whether he was talking to the guys who mopped the floors, with the managers who worked for him, with the women he expected to fall at his feet, or with the directors and vice presidents above him who would be working for him soon enough. He had come by his vanity honestly, as he had been supremely successful at everything he ever did, and he was the youngest person to hold the position he was now holding, Plant Manager, another step along his way to the summit. And he was a baller from Indiana.

Because of that when the call went out from the mysteriously designated coach, Marty Sennett, an older guy still hanging on to a white man's Afro in 1987, to put together a company team, he had no problem recruiting Jack Morton, a guy who had NBA potential until injuries forced him to fall back on the degree his many recuperations allowed him time to study for, and Tracy Morse, a former local San Diego high school star, and a few others who had played together before, and a new engineer, hired in the prior year, named Jimmy Williams, who said he could play, when Marty let them know the boss was on the roster.

At twenty-eight, Jimmy was the youngest player on the team, the only one under thirty, and still able to run without pain after not having played ball for over a year. The team dynamic and the coach's philosophy was based on Dan Martin being more important than the team, and therefore Dan had the green light to shoot the ball every time he touched it. Since he was a very good athlete and a streak shooter, he could carry the team when he was hot, but when he was not, he would keep shooting and the coach knew to keep his mouth shut. Jack would do his best to save them on Dan's two out of three cold nights, and Tracy was like a rec league Dennis Rodman, tireless and dogged under the boards even though undersized, defying his age, which no one knew for sure. They only knew he was older than everyone except the coach, and in the best shape of all of them. Since their real jobs and real lives came first for the thirty-somethings who made up the bulk of the team, the roster fluctuated game to game, and by the end of the season and the start of the Industrial League playoffs Jimmy was sixth man, coming off the bench to play small forward. His minutes had increased throughout the year, and in the one game Dan, Jack, and Tracy were all out of action Jimmy set the season scoring record for the team with 27, so by the last regular season game he was playing starter's minutes despite not starting. But when the team was at full strength they never wanted him to score, they wanted him to rebound. Other agendas were at play which mandated that being his role. What better opportunity, Jimmy rationalized, could there be to show he was a team player?

They cruised through the playoffs until they met a team in semi-finals that had beaten them before in a close game. Jimmy made two shots down the stretch that should have sealed it, but a certain boss did not have the temperament to dribble out the clock and kept shooting and missing, letting their opponents recover. It came down to the last minute, with Jimmy's SunRun squad inbounding the ball at half court, down by one. The ball was tossed to Jimmy, and no one picked him up for a couple of dribbles but then two men rushed him, making him pick up the ball before he wanted to. He spotted Jack under the basket and jumped to pass it to him, not a very fundamental thing to do, but these were desperate times. A defender stepped across Jack to shield him from the ball, but it was too late for Jimmy to change his mind, he could only angle the throw away from the impeding arm, high and hard, and hope Jack could catch it.

"Noooo!!" cried out Jack to stop the throw, but he couldn't push the ball back with his voice, he had to catch it. He jumped awkwardly along the baseline and reached up and snagged the ball. A pump fake, and a sweet kiss off the glass later, and SunRun had the lead.

One last miss, and then the last fifteen seconds could run off, but why did Tracy pass to Dan, and why didn't Dan pass it back? At least he was fouled before anything bad could happen. Surely a clutch player, and man upon whose shoulders the whole world would someday rest, would make the free throws and seal the deal. Jimmy took his position along the left lane line and assumed he wouldn't. He was going to short arm the shot and the ball was going to hit the front of the rim. The shot went up, pitifully short of the mark, and Jimmy leapt straight to where his premonition told him to go, and reached the ball before the startled defenders. As they surrounded him, he passed it back to Dan and the clock ran out.

The championship game was a farce, and like all great farces had a trick ending. SunRun was against a team, the Commodores, that had never had a close game all season. They had beaten SunRun by more than twenty points during their first meeting. They were younger, leaner, taller, quicker, and had the kind of stamina the SunRun players could only reminisce about. The rest of the squads were pissed the Commodores hadn't been forced into a more youthful level, since they weren't even working up a sweat against the other Industrial League teams. After fifteen minutes of the first half SunRun's starters were exhausted and deflated, and the score reflected it, down by fourteen and on the wrong end of two highlight reel slams. The coach threw in the towel, more or less, and put the second string out there to finish the half and at least get a workout. The only difference would be whether the final score was lopsided or very lopsided.

Jimmy looked around and saw he was the only guy who was even half decent at basketball on the court for SunRun, but he wasn't ready to give up. But when he saw what he had to work with, and what they were up against, he could see only one chance. They could not hope to handle this team if the pace was faster than a walk, nor could they handle the ball well enough to slow it down. They could not score inside nor stop their opponents from scoring inside at will. Maybe, just maybe, they could win a game of Horse against them?

So Jimmy dribbled down court and stopped far outside the three-point line and launched one. He hit the side of the rim, so it wasn't an air ball, but it was not even close to going in. The opposing players laughed as they had been laughing throughout the game and walked the ball up court instead of breaking. The first guy to get a pass past half court launched his own three. It sailed out of bounds without drawing any iron. His boys laughed so hard they forgot to play defense, and this time Jimmy pulled up at the three-point line and drained one. And now it was on. The guys who were ahead decided they were more than happy to join in a three-point shooting contest with the fat old men they were beating down anyway, so that was all they did for the rest of the half. They made one, and the old guys, Jimmy let the others try their luck after he made his, had 3. The fourteen-point lead had shriveled to eight before the horn blew. Jimmy launched another just after it sounded that dropped through after banking off the board that would have made it five if there had been a half a tick more left on the clock.

The second half was a lot tenser. In a game such as this a momentum swing can damage the psyche of a team faster than the weather can change on the prairie. Easy shots became challenges and free throws impossible dreams. The SunRun starters put in a valiant effort as the clock ticked away, but were down to fouling to keep some hope alive for the last five minutes of the game. For the younger team missing free throws became a pandemic, and they missed so many of them they lost track, and SunRun was able make a few shots to cut the deficit to one with only five seconds left. But that was all. The game was still lost. They had no choice but to foul, but even if the next free throw was missed there was no time to push the ball down court for a shot. But that was not to be the case, something far sillier happened. The free throw was indeed missed, and Tracy, who was the closest man to it, jumped to clear the board and heave the ball in desperation, but he didn't get the chance. The youthful leaper behind him reached over his back to take the ball away and knocked him down. There was no choice but to call the foul, and Tracy was gifted with the chance to win the game with one and one free throws.

Three seconds were left as Tracy calmly walked down the court. That was amazing because he was the only calm one in the gym. Everyone else was going nuts. Most of the spectators were players from other teams and assorted gym rats, and they were laughing and whooping in anticipation of witnessing how stupidly a game could be lost, and guys on one of the benches were cursing at each other while on the other they were dazed, saying things like, "Can you believe we might win this game?" There were a few young girlfriends cringing in the stands in anticipation of an angry night ahead.

Tracy stepped up and made both free throws as if he was in the gym by himself on a carefree summer's day. It happened so fast there was no time to savor them. As he danced around with the rest of the SunRun victors, Jimmy had no idea this would be the last championship party he would be part of in his basketball life. From this point forward the decline would be sharp. Children would come soon, and mortgages, and meetings lasting days and weeks, with countless hours squirming on airplanes and writhing through conference calls taking the place of sprinting and jumping as his recreation. But for now it was the time for toasts, for speeches and pats on the back. There was no reason to doubt the next year would be even better.

Three Pointers

At the beginning

First off it was a curve ball
I thought it would be high and tight.
It came on me and I was unaware
Of the total control of that bite.

Mental wrestling with no holds barred,
After two falls in a row I was sure.
Once again I had tripped over destiny's rope
Matching strength against strength to endure.

As it stands more progress could not have been expected
Although hope has its powers to enlarge,
Guess as long as I'm living, breathing, and coping
The will of my heart leads the charge.

The All-U championship game was an anti-climax, from the point of view of almost anyone watching or playing in it. But for Jimmy it was one long, continuous, voluptuous, orgasm from the opening tip to the final horn. The Goodfellas never trailed Pi-Kappa-Alpha, who had upset the Fog in the other semi-final, not for one second of the game. The defense was suffocating, and the offense was a shared buffet, with something for everyone. Hal and Darrell made the first baskets to put them up by four, and after Jimmy made the third shot the frat boys were never closer than four again. Any thoughts of a comeback or a let up in the second half were squashed with the opening tip, which floated lazily from Darrell to Jimmy, who just as leisurely dribbled up the left side of the court without being challenged. He calmly dribbled all the way to the base-line baffled by the fact no one seemed to be bothered enough to impede him. Then he turned and floated up for an easy lay in. He heard a familiar voice coming out of the darkness.

"Why not? If they're not gonna guard you!!" it sang out.

As he shrugged in the direction of the bodiless sound, Jimmy remembered where he heard that voice before. It was coming out of a dorm room in University Hall the day he was schooling Will one on one.

The Pi-Kappa-Alphas wilted after that shot, which put them down by ten. Their only hope had been to play zone, and being down double digits forced them out of it. They were able to close it to four mid-way through the second stanza, but by the time the clock read less than sixty seconds Tyrone was at the free throw line making the margin eight once again. As the first shot fell Jimmy started shaking hands with the guys on the bench, something Grassman was not happy about. He was coaching to the last whistle, and Jimmy had to keep focused, but in his mind, it was over. No way were any more points getting scored by the Greeks.

"This game is over. They won't score again!!" shouted Jimmy as the ball was played long and he raced to intercept it. He couldn't quite grab it, but this time he was not too tired to hustle until the last second ticked away, so he leaped and tipped it instead and it sailed out of bounds, giving all his mates a chance to set their defense. As Jimmy had promised, the score hadn't changed by the time the air horn blasted and the lines of congratulations began.

23. Remembered in the Past

I'm scared of old age
But I'm petrified of death –
Eighty years ago.

Once I saw an old man
Climbing the stairs,
And wished I could do as well.
(I was six months old at the time)

The year was 1900 and I am born,
On October 16,
A warm rainy day
And the air was so clean.
A man could be honest and still be proud!
But it was still all in the works.

I once felt in my heart exactly like you.
I ran rather than walked to my hideaways.
I was bold as I strolled at my ease.
Please…listen?
I've been like you; you will soon be like me –
Remembered in the past.

What do you feel in your heart now, old one?
Or does your heart float in a sea of memories?

I look to the future as always, young lord.
My grip slips daily, as does yours.
The sun will rise.

The second part of the Senior Presentation was to demonstrate the functionality of the systems each pair of students had designed to the professors they had studied under for the last four years. Twenty-five tables holding the projects of twenty-five teams were stationed around the big hall, held open to the public as well as the faculty who toured as a group, stopping at each table to bless or condemn the students' work. The calendar had changed to May and his adult life was only fourteen days from starting, and since even Papichulo was too nervous to talk as the two partners waited for the members of the faculty to reach their table, Jimmy's thoughts drifted to another day in early May when his life changed forever, when he was six years old.

Spring days when the sun shone proudly, firmly overcoming the winter chill still lurking in the darkness, were glorious to little boys who had been growing and fidgeting throughout the cold half of the year inside with their mothers and sisters. Each day when its warmth allowed them to run free there was a new adventure, a new challenge to be experienced around every corner. On this day a six-year-old Jimmy ran around the corner of the garage behind his house and found his brother, older than him by almost a decade, and his friends throwing a ball against the side of the garage, trying to fit it inside a metal rim. He watched, and watched, and watched and begged them to let him try, until they got so tired of playing and even more tired of hearing his cries they let Jimmy dance off the grass and onto the gravel. His brother put the ball in his hands and the group stood in a semi-circle to watch.

The ball was bigger than his head and seemed impossibly heavy to launch so high into the air, so he put the entirety of his tiny might into the heave, coiling his body around the ball and crouching down as low to the ground as he could without tipping over, the ball at the same elevation as his ankles. Then he used every inch of his body: ten toes and both feet and ankles and legs and arms and even his vocal cords, letting out a shout as he pushed the ball away with his entire being. And as he released it, his left wrist flicked, rolling the ball down his fingers to the tips, the nails, to give it that one last photon of energy, and he watched it beautifully rotate, rotate, up, up, and then fall back down, not quite reaching the height of the bottom of the net.

Those assembled laughed, enjoying the entertainment they had anticipated; but to Jimmy it was marvelous. The next one would be higher and then higher and then higher, and someday it would reach the rim, and some later day it would go in. He just knew it. They could laugh all they wanted. When they drifted away to go do whatever teenagers did when they weren't playing in the backyard, Jimmy had the gravel court to himself, the worn rubber ball to himself, and no one to tell him what he couldn't do if he continued to work at it, or to giggle in the corner when he tried and failed. The shy but bold flirtation initiating all love affairs had begun.

When the faculty members reached their table, Papichulo and Jimmy turned on the motor and oscilloscope and varied the motor torque. They all watched the screen as the saw tooth voltage output signal increased or decreased as the loop responded to the changes in input. As presented before, the motor could maintain the constant speed the loop was designed to control at low torques, but once the torque reached a certain point the speed decreased, which the mentors could not squabble over since it had been explained away beforehand. They wanted to, and the looks on their faces showed that, but they couldn't. All they had time to do was congratulate the pair and move on to the next table.

After their interrogators moved on the two young men turned and faced each other with the realization their academic journey was now complete. The Golden Ticket would soon be in their hands. Papichulo and Jimmy stood days away from becoming Bachelors of Science in the most highly anticipated career the future held, Electrical Engineering, on the cusp of the Electronic Age. Their success was assured. Soon they could go anywhere, do anything. An inner voice nagged at Jimmy there had to be a catch, but at this point, with his arm around the shoulders of his buddy and chuckling being the only sound his throat could make, he couldn't fathom what it was.

24. Isometric Iceman

By the end of the last week before the commencement ceremony the dorms had emptied except for the graduating seniors and a few other assorted students and the campus was easing into its summer hibernation. As each underclassman finished his or her last final exam they packed their cars or parents' cars and sped out of Peoria to start another summer break as quickly as possible, leaving only those who would be donning caps and gowns and walking across the stage on Saturday, May 16, to mill about the nearly deserted Yard. By Thursday night even the last party was held, as each person seemed to want to spend the last night of childhood alone or in small, private clusters and clutches, not wanting to take any chances of throwing up during the ceremony or oversleeping and missing it completely.

As he did on his first full day on campus, Jimmy strolled to the gym on his last full day. The contrast could not have been clearer. This time it was so empty each foot fall echoed as none of the dividers were in use, making it seem like an immense cavern. No mob of eager ballers filled it like on the first day. It took his eyes a while to adjust, but there were a few guys scattered around an immense man under the far hoop, and as he came closer Jimmy recognized the form of the afro and knew it was someone he had seen in the gym and played with before, Nate Tate. He had played on Bradley's varsity the year before Jimmy arrived as a freshman and had made a failed attempt to jump to the NBA the next, and still worked out at Haussler in hopes of catching on somewhere. A six-seven center was just not big enough, but he wasn't ready to admit that to himself yet, regardless of what the scouts told him, even though most everyone else could see it clearly.

"Now we've got enough!" called out another familiar player to Jimmy, one of the Kappa's, named Darius Jones. He was about six-four, six-six with his hair, and was known for dunking as happily and loudly as any mortal, but not like giant Nate Tate, who could really bring the house down.

As Jimmy looked around and counted, he added seven, plus himself. The teams were drafted, and before he even had a chance to work up a sweat, Jimmy was in the middle of a game of four on four half court, which had been insisted on by Nate, who refused to play full court, something about wanting to "save his knees" for an upcoming tryout. They had crossed paths before in Haussler, more than once, in fact, and it had been established Nate expected a high level of respect from small fry like Jimmy and Jimmy wasn't able to do that to the degree Nate could appreciate. In fact, Jimmy didn't respect him much at all. Nate was one of those guys who was bigger than everyone growing up and didn't have to work as hard as guys like Jimmy to be the star, and when he did climb to the level where his size was common, not extraordinary, he didn't have the love and devotion required to put in the work necessary to thrive in it. His expectation and receipt of the "star treatment" had not diminished however, and while six guys seemed honored to be selected to play in a pickup game with him, one was making sure he played opposite him, to have one last chance to imprint on Nate's mind that he didn't deserve it. To Jimmy he was the popular jerk who had the sweetest, most beautiful girl in school on his arm and took her for granted, refusing to open doors for her and always saying mean things, and for that he had to be punished.

The real reason, in Jimmy's mind at least, for Nate to play half court was so he could dominate the game and not have to work too hard. He was so much bigger than everyone else he could control the defensive board and keep his position under the basket on offense, and without the required wind sprints of full court the smaller men around him couldn't wear him down. As the next best players on the court, Darius and Jimmy sided with two others against Nate and three other no-names, and the game boiled down to Jimmy driving and scoring if Nate didn't stop him or dishing to Darius if he did, and Nate blocking shots, playing bully ball inside and dunking over everyone.

His team was up 6 to 5 when Jimmy drove the lane and put up a high arcing shot, higher than Nate could possibly block - except he did. The ball soared out of bounds.

"Goaltending!" shouted Jimmy, "Basket counts. Game over."

Nate chuckled. "No way was that goaltending, little man."

"No way you blocked that on the way up. It was coming down," responded Jimmy, once again, and for what Nate thought was going to be the last time, not showing the big man the proper respect.

He strode up to the smaller man and handed him the ball and said, "I'm not arguing with you. Just take the ball out and don't you dare come down the lane again."

Jimmy looked up but said nothing, because Nate had already told him what to say next. He took the ball at the top of the key and drove straight down the lane, charging directly at the huge beast heaving in anger in front of him and leapt without faking. Nate responded as the macho rules by which he lived dictated he respond, by gathering himself into a massive spring and uncoiling into the air to crush the ball as it rose toward the target, to splatter the ego of the pipsqueak who dared to challenge him in front of all those assembled, to give him the memory of one last humbling defeat to take with him into the darkness of adulthood.

As soon as Nate's feet left the ground he was helpless, and Jimmy knew he was helpless, in fact he knew he was helpless from the time he had issued his challenge. Another ego bigger than the brain it was housed in. Jimmy let go of the ball and dipped his shoulder to avoid the oncoming train. Darius was standing on the baseline, wondering how far the ball was going to get swatted when he saw it instead floating not toward the basket but on the perfect trajectory for him to leap up and catch it and take it along with him as he rose and throw it forcefully through the rim, just as Nate was turning in the air to reach for the ball that did not go where he had thought it was going, so not only did he not block it, his nose was inches away from the net as Darius rammed it home.

"Face!!" called out Darius before he could stifle it, as the other players reacted with derisive hoops that did not convey the kind of respect Nate was used to. Darius couldn't help but smile broadly even though he had never seen a man this big so angry. He had dunked many, many times before, but he could never remember doing it under circumstances like this over an almost NBA caliber player. It may be the best dunk of his life.

Jimmy was thinking ahead. "And that's game," he said. "Who's got next?"

Playgrounds and driveways, blacktop, concrete, and gravel, are like concert halls for hoops virtuosos, like garages for toddling musicians, like quarries for the sculptor. They are where crude blocks are chipped and sanded into masterpieces. Julius Erving was not transformed into Dr. J by a high school coach or the U Mass program but by the PhD he earned in Rucker Park, and that came only after attending many other cathedrals of learning, starting with the park across the street from the projects where he began his education. So like a world-famous jazz man loves to duck into a rundown after-hours speakeasy to jam until the sky is bright again, real ballers can make their magic equally in a stadium or a backyard, wherever the ball is tossed and a rim awaits it, and after the glory years of crowds and accolades, they come back to their asphalt roots to bounce and bank through their memories of younger days.

Jimmy's first job after college was in Indiana, and of course the subject of basketball came up amongst his new co-workers in the first few days, and it wasn't long before Jimmy was part of the Thursday Night Gremlin League, which was a group of guys the company photographer, Bill Grumman, who everyone including himself called Gremlin, gathered together in his backyard to play half court and drink beer afterwards. Bill had expanded the typical behind the garage court most houses in the Midwest had to the size of an elementary school half court and paved it with smooth cement, the perfect size for old guys who didn't have much to gain from running up and down a full court, and to whom "three- point range" pertained to the kitchen stove, not basketball. They drove directly from work and dressed in the basement before trotting out to the court to frolic.

Most of the guys had played in high school when their heads were still crowded with hair, and they knew the fundamentals of passing and shooting, spreading the floor, and talking and helping on defense, and the games were spirited and lively, while true ferocity was considered impolite. But all the elements that made the game art were there, with its links to the past of half hook shots and two-handed chest passes, and its latter-day innovations of behind the back dribbling and no look assists, and enough old-fashioned bragging and new-fangled insults to make both the winners and losers smile equally. The score was kept, but not remembered.

It was here that it came full circle for Jimmy, on this court, with these old guys whose backs always hurt for the next two days or for some other reason would be limping slightly, or sometimes not so slightly, as they walked in from the parking lot for work on Friday morning. Guys who took Tylenol for a day before playing, not after, because they knew it was going to hurt so why wait? Then they'd take more after, vowing to put their pain on layaway until another Thursday had passed.

This is what love truly is, and as Jimmy lie in the grass with a cold one, propped up on one elbow as he watched the last game wheeze its way to a close, he realized he didn't have it anymore. It was over, even though he would play out the string for the next few years without really investing the time to make the relationship work, but he wouldn't be out in someone's backyard at these guys' age popping pills to keep from screaming when he tried to move any body part, down to his eyelids, the next morning. The game had used him, and he'd used it, but it wasn't going to use him up. He wasn't going to be one of those guys with a limb or back that would never heal because he grasped too hard for too long at something that had let go of him long before to fend alone against the ravages of time.

No one was there to take next, of course, and Nate Tate refused to play another game with such inconsiderate and unappreciative opponents, and Jimmy's last game at Haussler Hall was over. As he sat, shoes off, leaning against the row behind him in the bleachers, he reflected on the many times he had sat in this very spot letting the endorphins wash into his bloodstream as his lungs steadily infused his arteries with deeply, slowly inhaled oxygen. As he wondered where the next chapter in his life would lead him, an older, familiar looking man walked out of the shadows of his consciousness and stopped in front of him.

"Hey," he said, breaking Jimmy's revelry, "You handle yourself very well out there. Are you a freshman?"

Something about the guy's hair, combed to the right side of his head like a greasy, artificial ski slope, was unmistakable, but Jimmy couldn't place him. "No sir, a senior," he replied. "I'm walking tomorrow with a BSEE."

"Well, congratulations," said the man.

He turned and walked away, carrying himself with a mix of pride and sadness. Jimmy remembered who it was; Joel Stowell, the longtime old school 1950's style coach of Bradley who had been fired to make way for the new school circus barker style of Dick Versace. It had been time for him to go, no doubt, but as these things often unfold, it had not been the most dignified departure. After all the glory, the fame, the wins and losses, he had been flushed out when the future did not favor the methods he had mastered and, like his coif, refused to tamper with. He had loved, had been loved, and was no longer loved by the game to which he devoted his life and made his career, leaving him only with his past as his present. Jimmy was left to wonder if his memories were fond or bitter.

Three Pointers

Isometric Iceman
Inventor of the sublime freeze
Mellow as coke on ice
He wonders why it has to hurt so bad
How it could be
The needle jumps the groove
On contact.

Nutritional Musician
Featherweight lyrics backed by conglomerate sound
Been on six or seven desks
Need whose expert opinion?
Just a melody from the frozen north.

Rats can jump
So climbing on chairs won't help
And so the Iceman and the Harmony Bringer must cling
As one -
Only then does he melt
Freezing his fear, faces the rat.

25. Blue Collar

A working man.
The job is the raft on the ocean
The hands are calloused sacrifices
The face is a living clock of human life
The mind full and resourceful,
Working to overcome the strife
In the form of an offspring
Or some ward.
And the working man would rise
Attempt the maze in full dress
As if someone had orchestrated the young champion
To slay the Minotaur.
The working man leans around corners,
Keeps steadily on the task.

May 16 was a beautiful day, from start to finish. As he made the short two block walk from his dorm room to the Fieldhouse along Main Street, the birds had never sung so sweetly, the warmth of the sun was never so perfect, even the cars screaming past with their honks and shouted insults at a man wearing a gown seemed cheery. The smile on his face had never been so sincere.

He woke up with the idea of writing a poem on this last day about graduating, something he began with, "If boredom is the soil in which creativity thrives, Peoria should be home to many great artists..." but throughout the day nothing else came out, like a turtlehead that never accomplished the task of becoming a full turd. What was the point anyway? He was not contemplating turning his life in a different direction. He was motoring down the road, literally, the next day toward the job he had trained for his whole life; as an analytical, technical, salaried with full benefits, corporate citizen. Poetry had no place in such an environment, not when the time for true frivolity was about to begin, when real women would replace the fantasies, exotic travel would replace adventure novels, and cars and money would never again not be in his possession. The spoils and riches of war were commencing to fall into his open chest, and wasting time teasing words into sonnets of passion and pleading would be counterproductive at best.

There was mingling to be done as they found their places in line for the procession. Jimmy toyed with the idea of announcing to the assembled throng that it was indeed he who had written all the poems delivered in dark passageways on moonless nights over the past months, but never seriously considered it. Again, what would be the point? If he hadn't exploited their magic for his own ends before today, what good would it do anyone now? Instead he maneuvered himself along with Papichulo to the end of the line of diploma recipients, so they would be the very last ones to cross the stage and flip their tassels to the side marking the end of their college lives. As they shuffled their way silently toward the podium, a memory from a past validation came to Jimmy's mind.

When Jimmy was summoned to his mother's sewing table it was usually not for a pleasant chat. His best hope was for a scolding that did not lead even more unpleasantness. His mother valued the scraps of time she had for her hobby-turned-necessity, as mending clothes and adding patches was the only way to keep her brood covered, so when she stopped her bobbin to turn to him this time he knew he had made some transgression but couldn't fathom what it was. He had picked up the clothes in his room. He had finished his homework. He had eaten all his vegetables and wiped the plates dry after his sister had washed them. All before running to the backyard to play basketball with his brother, home on leave from the Army, the first time he had come back since Jimmy had joined the seventh-grade basketball team and on his birthday had added a "teen" to the back end of his age.

Slugger had enlisted four years before, when Jimmy was only nine, and whenever he came home they played whichever sport, baseball or football, was in season, so he could gauge where his little brother was and help him along. To Jimmy that was not the reason they played, it was so he could show his older brother how much bigger and better he was than the last time he saw him. Having his brother leave was not heart breaking for Jimmy, in fact he breathed a sigh of relief when his brother packed his bags and left him with a bedroom to himself. No more torture. But there was no one in the world he wanted to show off his burgeoning skills to more than him, and this time it was basketball, a game they had never played seriously before and Slugger had taught him next to nothing about.

The stern words which came out of her mouth were like being back-handed a bachelor's degree in Hoops Devotion. "Your brother came and talked to me about you," she said slowly and calmly, a sign she was irritated and trying not to yell.

"Oh?" asked Jimmy. They were in the middle of a game of one on one, and at thirteen Jimmy was no match for his twenty-two-year-old sibling, but he hadn't made a fool of himself by any stretch. Anyway he hadn't thought he had until his brother abruptly walked off the court. His older sibling had been trying to show him how to dribble the ball right handed or how to release his jump shot, or something, and Jimmy was trying to show Slugger what he already knew and had no patience or desire to learn anything. He just wanted to play.

"He's very frustrated with you," she continued. "He says you are really, really, good at basketball, but the trouble is you know it. You won't listen to what he's trying to teach you."

Jimmy didn't care about a word she said after "basketball." It was the last one he needed to hear. All the other sports he played were ones Slugger had taught him how to play. This one was different. He had learned to play without his older sibling's guidance, after he had left him to fight off their sisters by himself, and learned well enough to frazzle him into whining to their mother about it. Once this epiphany was experienced there was no way he would ever listen to his brother when it came to his new love, basketball. He could and would make this relationship work on his own. All he had to do was develop what God had given him and let his body grow into the manhood it was destined for. No one, not his family, his friends, those in authority looking down on him, not even those whose talents he could never hope to match, could take it away from him. He knew how to love and to rejoice in its blessings, and his days would be enriched by his boldness. His life would not be lived on the sidelines, and there was nothing more he could ask for.

Jimmy was the last one to cross the stage and be handed his diploma. He was so hoarse from hollering at those proceeding him he had no voice left and could only communicate with a grin when he lifted his free hand, the one without the tube in it, to flip the braids from left to right. There were handshakes and pictures and kisses from grandmothers, and as the sun fell behind the buildings surrounding the quad an eerie silence filled Jimmy's heart. Another phase of life had expired, the next was beginning its march toward extinction, and for every matter he had settled two more were unsettled. It was now clear time does not proceed into a funnel, it expands into ever widening uncertainty with each second of its passing. It is we who dwindle. Jimmy packed his bags and drove off into the future the next morning with the conviction he would never look back on any of the regrets remaining concealed in the campus of his soul. Not with so many moves left to make and games to play.

www.ingramcontent.com/pod-product-compliance
Lightning Source LLC
Chambersburg PA
CBHW022201050726
47590CB00002B/601